THE MAITLAND HOUSE CHRONICLES

Volume 1

MAGGIE NASH

Copyright

For more information, or to book an event, contact :
Email :maggie@maggienash.com
http://www.maggienash.com

Cover design by Paula Roe

ISBN - Paperback: **978-0-6453652-2-1**
First Edition : February 2024

Books by the Author

Also by Maggie Nash

The Master's Prize

Kinky Bet

The Dream Master

The Relic

Crash and Burn

The Maitland House Chronicles

    Anna

    Gemma

And by Maggie Mitchell

Chasing Terpsichore

Calling Calliope

Moonshadow

THE MAITLAND HOUSE
CHRONICLES

I

ANNA

I

Chapter One

London, April 10, 1816

She expected a man.

Instead, a tall woman stood just inside the open door of Maitland House. She could have been in her late twenties or perhaps she was nearer to forty in years, it was difficult to tell. She had the look of a Botticelli angel with her pale, flawless skin, and flowing strawberry blonde tresses. A stark contrast to herself, with her dark brown mop of wild curls and rosy complexion.

"Ah, you are Anna," she said, her voice warm and welcoming. "You have come to Maitland House to be *Awakened*. We have been expecting you."

The woman stepped back and gestured for Anna to enter. "Come in so that you may begin your journey."

Anna's heart stopped. *How could this woman know anything about me?* "I have come to speak with Alexandr Sakarov. How do you know my name? I told no one my identity when I arranged this meeting. Not even Mr. Sakarov."

She smiled and glided towards the elaborately carved staircase across the large entrance hall. "Come this way, the Master awaits your company. He will answer all your questions."

Anna followed, her eyes glued to the stairs as they curved upwards, disappearing behind a wall of panelled timber.

She continued to speak as they climbed the staircase. "I imagine this is all very strange to you, but soon you will find what you seek, and all will be well."

These words echoed in her mind. Would she find what she was seeking? *Do I have the courage to try?* Despite the coldness of the late autumn evening, unfamiliar heat touched her in forbidden parts of her body, and her unbound nipples tightened as they scraped against the roughness of the raw silk shirt she'd been instructed to wear.

Strange men will touch my body.

She shivered, feeling wicked for even entertaining the thought. Could she go through with this?

How could she not? Her body told her what her mind refused to acknowledge. She could no longer pretend she didn't want this...didn't crave it. Erotic dreams of unfulfilled passion left her confused and with an ache she hadn't the faintest idea how to soothe. So, it wasn't surprising that when she overheard hushed whispers of this place and what she could experience here, she found herself compelled to investigate and discover what she craved.

* * *

Justin Black paced the room as he waited for the woman he loved to arrive. He had good reason to be anxious, as his friend Alexandr Sakarov was a man of hedonistic pleasures who offered an exotic service. For those with the money to indulge, women and men came for their innermost fantasies to be fulfilled within these walls. Most of the clientele were men, both married and single, who did not wish the complication of a mistress, or married women who wanted to explore their sexuality away from boring husbands and the eyes of society. But on occasion single women would apply, as had Anna Chamberlain. The woman he intended to marry.

These women came for what Alexandr had named an *Awakening*. This consisted of one week spent in an introduction to the art of sensuality. Most women who applied were past marriageable age. Spinsters who realized their chances to experience pleasure were slipping away, and perhaps this was the case with Anna. At twenty-seven, she was almost a spinster's age by society's standards, and had spent many years caring for her elderly parents, but to Justin she was still the young innocent girl he had fallen in love with all those years ago.

There was no doubt in his mind she fully intended to be initiated into the pleasures of the flesh one way or another. She had always been stubborn and once she set her mind on something, she did not falter until she achieved her goal. It was one of the reasons she had clashed so often with her parents all those years ago, and also why they had sent her away when they feared he would corrupt her innocence.

He smiled. Perhaps they were right. However, his intentions had always been honorable. He had always wanted to marry her.

Eventually.

Thank God he'd been able to convince Alexandr to let him be the man to take her virginity. He'd wanted her since he was eighteen years of age, and now this chance to claim her as his own had literally fallen into his lap. He only hoped she would forgive him when she discovered the identity of her first lover.

Footsteps sounded in the distance and Justin looked towards his friend sitting behind his desk, sipping red wine. Alexandr's brown eyes twinkled with humour. "Do not worry, my friend. I will look after her."

Justin smiled. "That's not what I fear Alexandr. Just don't enjoy yourself too much."

Alexandr laughed. "So, tell me does Anna know of your exotic predilections?"

Justin threw back his glass and drained the last of his drink. "No, she does not. That's the reason why I am allowing you and your staff to prepare her. I'm not sure she would be so open to my tastes if I were the first to initiate her. Despite her desire to participate in the activities of your house, she is a complete innocent and the last time we spoke, she believed me to be as innocent as she. We have shared only the most chaste of kisses and that was when we were mere children."

Alexandr grinned. "Very well then, but don't be alarmed by what you see and hear in this room or any of the chambers, Justin. I know she is special to you, but my guests come here to discover their inner sexuality. Everything I do is to keep them aroused at all times. I will, however, honour your special request. She will remain virgin in all ways that matter until she is prepared for you. I have your instructions, as well as her letter outlining her own requests. Until she is ready, you may watch her preparation from our viewing areas if that is what you wish. That should get you in the mood quite nicely, I would think."

"This is allowed?"

"Of course, I'll allow it, but you must leave this room now or Anna will see you before she is ready."

The soft knock on the door startled him into action. "Yes, indeed. I'll wait in your inner office while you meet with her. Be gentle—she has no idea what she has let herself in for."

Alexandr stood and held the door, ready to close it behind him, "Trust me Justin. I know what I'm doing."

Justin sighed. *Why does this statement not give me any comfort?*

* * *

A deep voice answered the soft knock on the door.

"Come in Cassandra."

Anna's breathing became erratic, and she would have passed out had her companion not held out her hand and helped her into the room.

"Breathe," Cassandra whispered, urging her forward.

She heard the voice speak again. "Ah, I see you have brought our guest. Splendid. That will be all, Cassandra."

Anna held fast to her, pleading with her eyes for her to stay. She smiled sympathetically at her, but slowly withdrew her hand.

"Everything will be as wonderful as you imagined. I will see you soon. Don't worry."

Anne sucked in a breath, trying so very hard to be as brave as she'd been when she had asked her maid to arrange this adventure. She was here to be awakened to pleasure, and everything she'd heard about Alexandr Sakarov said he was an honorable man, but now it was about to happen, her heart wouldn't stop thundering. She turned to face him, and her mouth went dry. He was a very handsome man. She felt a blush of heat surge within her at the sight of his tall muscular build and rakish long dark hair hanging in wild waves just below his shoulders. The tanned skin of his forearms contrasted with the pure white silk of his shirt as he held out his large but elegant hand.

"Please relax, Anna," he said. His voice, with the smooth tone of his faint Russian accent gently coaxing her to calm down, although it would take more than this to stop her heart from racing. "Nothing will happen here unless you wish it. With only one word you can refuse any touch or any game. This is all about your pleasure."

Game? Anna took his hand, sighing as her body heat surged, and allowed herself to be drawn further into the room. Behind her the door closed and she was now alone with this man who would introduce her into a world of pleasure where her fantasies would come to life. Taking a deep breath, she squeezed his fingers before letting go, and looked directly into his hypnotic brown eyes.

His nostrils flared and the corners of his mouth kicked up as he chuckled. "Ah...I see you are more relaxed now. This is good. After all, your experience here is to be an education, not a punishment." His face lit up with a wicked grin. "Unless, of course, you *wish* to be punished."

What? Her heartbeat quickened. *Why would I wish to be punished?*

His fingertip traced a line across her cheek, resting under

her chin tilting her face towards him, forcing her to gaze into his eyes. "Don't worry *milaya moya*, my sweet. We will teach you how to experience pleasure, and you *will* enjoy it."

Oh my. Her insides quivered but she wasn't sure if it was the light feel of his skin on her own, or the implied eroticism of his words. It was of no consequence because either circumstance saw her holding her breath in anticipation. She had spent many hours reading stories she knew were forbidden to a lady of her station, books she had secretly acquired and hidden from the judgemental eyes of her parents. She'd never dreamed the sensations described within those erotic stories would be so intense or induce so many different physical reactions when experienced in reality.

All he did was touch my face with one fingertip.

As he released her, Anna's breath quickened to such an extent she gasped for air. Her mind reeled with the anticipation of the wonders awaiting her, if her reaction to a light touch and a few words was an example of what was to come.

Alexandr leaned against his desk with his legs crossed, his expression stern. "Are you naked under your clothing?"

She lifted her head and met his eyes, bewildered by the harsh tone of the question. "Excuse me sir?"

Alexandr's voice, though still calm, took on a more commanding tone. "I did not ask a difficult question Anna. Do you or don't you have any undergarments under your dress?"

Was this a test to see if she had followed his instructions? She swallowed a large breath and let it out as slowly as she dared. "I have nothing but skin against the raw silk, as you requested sir."

His gaze heated as they swept over her body from her

head to her feet and then back again. "Then you won't mind proving that to me."

"Wh—what?"

"You do wish to be awakened, do you not, Anna?"

"Yes," she whispered, although at that precise moment, the reality of what she was doing had begun to dawn on her and she wasn't at all sure. However, she was beginning to feel that things had progressed too far to go back, and the thought of leaving without accomplishing what she had come for was not something she wanted to think about.

"Good. Then you will undo the front fastenings of your dress and show me that you have complied with my instructions."

Without thinking, she responded to his commanding tone as her fingers fumbled with the first ribbon. Her face heated as he watched her shaking hands while they struggled to comply with his order. When the last tie was undone, she dropped her hands to her sides and waited for his next move. When she lifted her eyes, it was to find Alexandr standing so close she could feel the heat of his body against her bare skin, and her nostrils filled with a musky masculine scent.

She could not stop the small gasp as his warm breath washed over her face when he spoke, his words quiet, but with an undertone of command she did not quite understand.

"Your first lesson, my little friend, is to obey me without question. Do you understand?"

Before she had a chance to answer he grabbed both sides of the gown and slipped them off her shoulders, exposing her whole body to him.

Her nipples sharpened to points and her nether regions

throbbed as she desperately tried to pull the sides of the gown back together.

"What are you doing?" she whispered.

Alexandr's voice was gentle, but his hands remained firm on her garment.

"Do not fight me, Anna. I am merely reminding you that your body is nothing but an instrument for your own pleasure. You need not be ashamed. From what I can see you have a body most women would covet, and many men would move mountains to worship."

The embarrassment faded only a small amount, to be replaced by a tingling, which spread over her body when he released her garment and cupped her breasts in his warm hands. Her eyes closed and she gasped as his thumbs and forefingers squeezed the peaked tips in exquisite torture.

"Ah...you will be a pleasure to teach...so sensitive and so responsive." Abruptly, he stopped and eased the sides of her gown back together. "My servants will take you to your room now and prepare you for the night. I know you will have pleasant dreams, my little friend."

He lifted her hand to his lips and kissed it before turning away, dismissing her. "Until tomorrow, when the real enjoyment begins."

The door opened and two young men came into the room and took their places either side of her. Anna lowered her head as she retied the gown, but when she lifted her face Alexandr had gone.

The first man, an angelic-looking blond with pale blue eyes took her arm. "Come with us Anna, we will accompany you to your room."

She nodded and turned as the other man, as dark as his companion was fair, led the way through the door.

* * *

Alexandr smiled as he closed the door to his outer office. "She is certainly a beauty Justin...and so responsive too. You are to be congratulated on your excellent taste."

Justin felt himself scowling. He was beginning to regret his decision to watch the preparation. "You certainly seemed to be enjoying yourself. What made you stop?"

"Yes, she has exquisite breasts, and one of the most beautiful bodies I have seen."

"Alexandr, be careful what you say here."

"Do not worry Justin. I must admit she is tempting, but I did not forget to whom she belongs. I made a promise to you. You should have more trust in our friendship."

He tightened his hands into fists, tapping them at his sides. He must try harder to control his jealousy. If he was to achieve his goal, he had to maintain his distance and allow Anna to be awakened to her desires. Only then could he initiate her and claim her for his own. He had waited ten years; he could wait another few days. "I am sorry Alexandr, I do trust you. It is difficult watching the woman I love being touched by another man."

"Do you want to put a stop to it? Tell her you want to marry her and take it from there?"

"I wish I could, but it has been too long since we last saw each other, and heaven knows what stories her parents told her about me. No, since she sought this place out, I must allow her to experience what she desires. The fact that she chose to be here gives me hope that she has the passion to

THE MAITLAND HOUSE CHRONICLES · 13

enjoy the type of pursuits I have in mind. I must allow this week to unfold the way she wishes, and pray she still has feelings for me."

"Ten years is a long time, my friend. People change. *You* have changed. She may not be the same person you remember."

"I realize that, Alexandr. However, the woman I saw to-night is even more alluring to me than the girl I left all those years ago. The courage she has shown in defying her upbring-ing to come here shows me that she is becoming the woman I always knew she would be. My perfect mate. After seeing Anna with you in that room, I feel more confident than ever I made the right choice in waiting for her to be prepared before I make my presence known. She will never forgive me if I deprive her of the chance of a lifetime...to have all her fantasies fulfilled. In truth, I plan for this to be the only time she is ever seen or touched by another man. After this week she is mine, and mine alone."

Alexandr smiled. "Very well my friend, if you are certain then we will begin the training tomorrow. Do you wish to stay in one of our guest rooms for this week?"

"Thank you but no. I'll return to my house so as not to raise suspicion amongst my staff. The last thing I need is gossip associated with my marriage to Anna, and we all know how servants speak. That's how I was made aware of this circumstance, and it is only because I have known Anna's servant since I was a child that I trust her not to gossip. I'll return in the morning to view her progress from your private viewing points."

"As you wish. Are you sure you are comfortable watching

the proceedings tomorrow? You know what the initial training session, involves after all."

Justin tightened his grip on the stem of the wine glass and placed it onto the table. "Indeed, I am very aware, but I find that like a moth drawn to a bright light, I cannot look away. I will be here."

"Then I wish you a pleasant night's sleep my friend."

2

Chapter Two

Sleep did not come easily for Justin as he relived the moment he first caught sight of Anna as she'd arrived at Alexandr's house. She was even more striking than he remembered. Not a traditional beauty by any means, in fact many would find her wild, curly hair less than perfect and her full red lips not quite feminine, but to Justin these features made her all the more alluring. He closed his eyes and pictured her body as Alexandr had bared her to his gaze.

She is magnificent.

He had been in a state of constant arousal from the minute her clothes parted, giving him the view he had fantasized about since his first hormonal rush as a boy.

But it wasn't just her body he craved. He loved the passion she showed in everything she experienced. They had just realized their feelings for each other when her scheming parents had found them kissing and shipped her off to Europe. Nothing less than a duke would be good enough for their daughter, and the likes of him would never be allowed to ruin her chances for a successful marriage. As a second son from a lesser family, Justin didn't even come close to fulfilling their greedy expectations.

Those first months had been hell. Her leaving had left a large hole in his life that had never been filled. None of his letters ever reached her and after they were returned, he knew her parents would never allow her to see him, let alone tell him where she was.

He had removed himself to the continent for several years, not wanting to hear any news of her impending marriage, but never once had he given up on the possibility of finding her again. He had recently returned to London for one of his infrequent visits, and it was only through luck that Anna's servant remembered him and sought his help. She'd found out what Anna had planned and was worried for her mistress. Given that the laws regarding lewd behaviour had severe penalties, her worry was more than warranted. She had approached him at his townhouse, chancing that he would be willing to help keep her mistress safe. Up until that moment he'd assumed she'd been married off to some elderly peer and waiting for widowhood. Now with her parents no longer alive to interfere, and with this current situation falling into his lap, he felt fate was finally smiling on him. There was no way he was letting this opportunity slip through his fingers. She would be *his*, and this time *no one* could stop it from happening.

He smiled as he lay on his bed and stared at the ceiling. This was going to be a difficult week, but the prize at the end would be worth every minute of torment.

* * *

The two young men led Anna to another wing of the house, several corridors distant from Alexandr Sakaroff's office. The dark-haired man stopped in front of an ornately carved door at the end of a hall. He opened the door and lit the lamp on a side table just inside the room. Anna followed him in at the urging of the blond whose firm hand on the small of her back nudged her forward.

Anna gasped as she alked into the chamber that was to be her room for the next week. There were several oriental paintings covering the walls. All were exquisite works of art, but their content hocked her. The scenes depicted men and women engaging in all kinds of sexual acts. Many she would never have thought possible in her wildest dreams, despite her secret education. Her mouth opened, not able to stop herself from staring at the largest painting on the wall opposite the large four-poster bed. A naked woman knelt with her head and arms resting on a table covered with folds of golden silk. A naked man stood behind her, as if thrusting into her. Her head was thrown back and on her face was a picture of pure ecstasy. As the woman was being pleasured by one man her eyes locked with another, who sat fully clothed in a carved chair across the room watching this most intimate of acts. Anna's face heated she put herself in the place of the woman. Would that be one of the scenes she would experience? Would she allow it? She was no longer sure what she would do. She had discovered a heightened sense of awareness from the minute she had removed her undergarments and wrapped herself in the roughened raw silk as Alexandr Sakaroff had instructed her.

Another door opened, and the dark-haired man disappeared through it.

"James prepares your bath," the blond man said. "You must remove your clothes now."

Anna clutched the edges of her gown closer to her body. "I can manage on my own quite well thank you."

The blond angel, whose name was still a mystery, answered her with a hint of a smile in his voice. "Of course, you are able to, but if you are to be properly prepared for your *Awakening*, you must become accustomed to others seeing your body. It is a rule the Master has set for all."

Oh? "I do not think so."

"Take a deep breath my child. You can do this." The soft feminine voice came from behind her. "It is something you want for yourself and to achieve your goal you must comply. No one outside of this house will know. And nothing besides your bath and personal preparation will happen tonight."

Anna turned to find Cassandra entering her room. She placed a filmy *peignoir* on the bed and signalled the remaining man to go into the bathroom.

"I am not sure I am ready for this. It's more overwhelming than I expected."

"What did you expect to find here Anna?"

Anna turned away as Cassandra unfastened the ties of the gown. It was a fair question. What had she thought would happen here? "I did not think too much on the details, only the outcome."

Cassandra took her hand and drew her towards the bathroom where the scent of sandalwood and patchouli wafted through the door. "Then you agree you wish to become a woman awakened?"

When they entered the bath chamber, both men stood behind Anna and slid her gown off her shoulders before she even realized what was happening.

"Oh my..."

Cassandra smiled. "Step into the bath Anna. Darius and Jamie will assist you. There is nothing to fear. You will feel only pleasure."

Biting her lip, Anna decided to conquer her fear. Her body was tingling, and she felt a growing dampness between her thighs. *Is this why I came here?*

She lifted her foot and stepped into the warm, fragrant water. As Cassandra let go of her hand, the man known as Jamie poured a pitcher of warm water over her shoulder. As she felt it cascading over her breasts, Darius rubbed a sweet-smelling substance over his hands and then massaged it into the skin of her back. His nimble fingers moved over her neck and shoulders rubbing the fragrant soap into her tense muscles. She sighed and closed her eyes, unable to stop herself enjoying the sensation as he continued to work his magic. Another pair of hands touched her breasts, and she cried out not in pain, not in embarrassment, but with something very different.

Pleasure. *Is this what desire feels like?*

Never in her life had a male seen her unclothed, and here she was standing naked in front of two strange men. To her surprise she was not as bothered by it as she thought she would be. In fact, she found that she might very much enjoy being seen and touched by these beautiful men.

What is happening to me? Am I wanton?

Her skin burned as both men soaped over her with efficiency. She tingled with sensations she had never before felt. Not brave enough to open her eyes, she allowed herself to enjoy the experience and remind herself this was why she had come. She wanted to experience pleasures of the flesh, and indeed her journey thus far had not disappointed her.

After finishing her bath, Anna was wrapped in a thick blanket and told to lie on her back on a cushioned table that had been set up in front of the fire in the main bedroom. Relaxed and in a sensual haze, she complied without argument until she felt her legs being opened and placed either side of the table and the blanket folded back over her waist.

"What are you doing? Let me go!"

She struggled to get off the table, but Cassandra sat behind her head and clasped her hands in place. "Do not worry. The boys will now finish your preparation. It is nothing to fear."

She struggled to imagine what other preparation they had in mind with her legs splayed and the intimate parts of her body so exposed. Before she could protest again, a warm towel was placed over her mound. She gazed over at one of the paintings she realized what they were about to do, increasing her efforts to gain her freedom.

"No! I will not be cut."

Jamie leaned over her waist and held her firmly the table. "You must trust us, Miss Anna. This is also what the Master has ordered. Everyone who comes to this house must

acquiesce with his orders. I promise it will add to your pleasure, and that of your lovers."

"You will not mark me?"

Cassandra spoke softly. "There are no blades Anna, only a
special ointment brought to us from Persia. It will denude the
hair from your woman parts without discomfort. You must
trust us when we tell you, all you experience while you are
here in this house will be pleasurable."

"But—"

"Relax and close your eyes. Try to imagine the man
you dream of is watching while you are being touched so
intimately. Your body is being prepared for him, so he may
worship you."

"How did you know I dreamed of a man?"

Cassandra smiled. "All who seek *Awakening* here at Maitland House have a special man they dream of, whether he be
living, or fantasy. Use that fantasy, Anna. Let it wrap itself
around you and fuel your pleasure."

The warm sensual tone of her voice soothed Anna as she
closed her eyes and attempted to relax. The warm towel was
replaced by a pair of nimble fingers smoothing a cool ointment over her curls. She took Cassandra's advice and called
up an image. In her mind she saw the man who haunted her
dreams. The man she always saw, but he had been lost to her
for many years. He was probably long married by now, and
had forgotten all about her, however she could never let go
of the look in his eyes as he'd lowered his head to kiss her,
or the firmness of his shoulders as she'd clung to him while
he had changed her world with just one touch. Shaking her
head, she tried to put his image out of her mind. There was

no point wishing for the impossible. He'd left her and never looked back. This was why she was here, to let go and allow others to enlighten her on the pleasures of the flesh. Now she was finally free of the bonds of her family, she wanted to experience a sexual experience for herself.

The hands gently but firmly rubbed over her intimate folds as the cream heated her skin, causing a pleasant tingling. Another warm towel draped over her and one of the men wiped the ointment off in long strokes. She shivered as a warm breath blew over her folds. Her eyes opened and Darius winked as he closed her legs and replaced the blanket over her.

Later, finding herself ensconced in the big comfortable bed and more relaxed than she could ever remember, she thought about all the liberties she had allowed these strange but beautiful people to take with her body. She held her breath as one of her fingers made its way across the bare skin between her legs. She imagined herself as the woman in the painting on the wall, her skin smooth and creamy and exposed for both men who knew all her body's most intimate secrets. She felt very wicked. She let out that breath and smiled before drifting off to a sleep that promised dreams of the pleasurable acts to come.

* * *

Anna woke to a swish of curtains and a beam of warm sunlight across her face. She opened her eyes, and blinked a few times, taking in her unfamiliar surroundings.

"Good morning, Anna," a soft voice greeted her.

She squinted but couldn't make out the face that went

with the voice. Pushing herself up on her elbows, she moved up the bed to gain a better view. She smiled as Cassandra handed her a cup of steaming hot chocolate.

Looking down, she saw her naked breasts as they peeked out over the edge of the bedding. She gasped as the cool morning air teased them like fingers tenderly pulling on the sensitive tips.

Exactly like last night when Jamie...

Blushing, she pulled back the bedding to cover herself.

Cassandra laughed. "You will soon be used to baring more than just your breasts, young Anna. Have you forgotten your preparations from last evening already?"

The heat in Anna's face intensified as memories of the previous night flooded back. Oh my, she definitely had not forgotten.

Cassandra sat on the edge of the bed and took hold of one of Anna's hands, stroking the delicate skin on the inside of her wrist. "Did you not enjoy the attentions of Darius and Jamie? They will be most disappointed to hear you were dissatisfied."

"N-no..." she stammered, shuffling a little under the bed-clothes to steady herself. "It was most...pleasing." She closed her eyes, remembering the sensations. *They were so gentle.* "It is so very different to everything I am used to, is all."

Cassandra's blue eyes met hers. "Do not fear Anna. It is not unexpected that these experiences can be overwhelming at first. Especially for a young lady of your station who has led such a sheltered life. Are you very certain you wish to continue with your *Awakening*? You are not a prisoner here. You must always remember that you may leave at any time."

"Oh yes," she answered without hesitation. "More than ever, I want to be *Awakened*." Her insides tingled in anticipation of what the next few days held in store for her. She really *did* want this. Her body yearned for it.

Cassandra smiled and stood. "That is good news. You will not regret your decision. Now finish your drink for there is much to be done today."

Taking one last sip of the delicious chocolate, Anna handed the cup back to Cassandra. "Can you tell me what to expect today?"

Cassandra shook her head. "No, I cannot. The effect is not as powerful if you have warning of what is to come."

Her heart stopped. "'Warning'?"

Cassandra's lips twitched. "Do not worry, you'll find it quite pleasurable. Some of our clients have told us this part of the preparation is the most enjoyable of all. " She held her hand out to her and helped her out of the bed.

As her feet hit the floor the door opened, and Darius and Jamie appeared.

Her hands flew to cover her bare mound and her breasts.

Both men smiled. Darius took a step forward and pulled her hands away from her body.

"You must not cover yourself, Miss Anna. The Master wishes to see you all of you now and he will be displeased that you have not complied with his wishes."

Cassandra nodded as Anna looked to her for guidance. All right. She could do this. She *wanted* to do this. Taking a deep breath, she stood taller, pushing her breasts out and causing their peaks to tighten in anticipation of what was to come.

Jamie moved forward and raised a hand. Anna held her

breath as he circled one nipple with a gentle caress of his index finger. Her nipples tightened almost painfully.

"So beautiful isn't she, Darius?" said Jamie.

"Yes, and so responsive too," said Darius. "It will be a pleasure to prepare her for her *Awakening*."

Anna blushed. They were discussing her as if her body did not belong to her, and she was surprised to find she as reacting to such talk. She felt wanton, wicked, and wanted all at the same time. That strange feeling deep inside at the tip of her womb was back. Desire? If this was desire—then she wanted more.

Cassandra frowned at the two men. "We must take Anna to the Master. Lead on gentlemen."

Both men stood back and bowed before turning and leading the way out of the room.

"Forgive them for being so forward, Anna. They truly appreciate a beautiful woman, and they forget that they must keep control of themselves."

Anna found herself smiling. How could she be angry with them? *They think that I am beautiful.* "Don't worry Cassandra. It is of no consequence. I don't find it unpleasant to be told I am pleasing to the eye."

Cassandra took her hand and led her along the corridor. "I cannot disagree with you there, but both of them are aware that no man is to touch you from now on, unless the Master allows it. They were disobeying orders."

"It was only a gentle touch, and there was no harm done. Please do not worry Mr Sakaroff with such a trivial matter."

"The Master," said Cassandra.

"I beg your pardon?" Anna stopped walking, trying to understand what she had just heard.

"The Master. You must now refer to Mr. Sakaroff as the Master until your preparation is complete."

"But why must I do that? I am not a slave, and you have reminded me I am not a prisoner here."

A hint of amusement lit Cassandra's eyes. "You may not be a prisoner here, but you may well find yourself a slave to the pleasures of the flesh."

* * *

Anna's face flamed all over again as they reached their destination. Alexandr Sakaroff stared dispassionately while he inspected her naked body.

"Come and stand in front of me, Anna, so that I may see your preparations were carried out as I instructed."

The heavy rhythm of her heart beat a cacophony in her head. She tried lifting one foot to move forward, but her leaden leg would not comply. She heard the door close behind her and turned her head to see she was now alone with the man she was told to call "Master".

A voice sounded from across the room. "I am waiting."

She flinched, turning back as her legs, of their own volition, propelled her to stand where she'd been ordered.

"Cassandra instructed you with the manner in which to address me?" said Alexandr, his slight accent and deep voice sending tingles all over her skin.

She met his gaze, staring into his soft brown eyes and nodded. "Yes..." she gasped, her lungs depleted of air and in need of replenishment. Alexandr frowned, one of his eyebrows lifting.

Gulp. She could do this. She *wanted* to do this.

Alexandr turned away and started walking towards the door.

"Yes Master."

He stopped, turning back towards her, and smiled. "That was difficult for you wasn't it little one," he asked.

She could only nod, her mouth so dry her tongue appeared stuck.

"This is good. A little resistance makes the acquiescence all the sweeter," he said. He walked back to her and took her hand. "Come with me and we will begin the adventure."

Her eyes met his and she relaxed. All she saw was warmth and a hint of humour. She instinctively knew she had nothing to fear from this man. He led her behind a curtain and to a comfortable chair. It was a grandfather design upholstered with soft brown leather and he instructed her to sit.

"The leather will be cold on your skin, but you will adjust quite soon. I'll have Darius tend the fire to make sure you do not catch a chill."

Confused, she started to speak, but Alexandr placed a finger over her lips. "Before you speak, remember the first rule I gave you last evening?"

Anna closed her eyes, picturing their first meeting. She recalled the words he used while he stripped her gown from her shoulders and her skin heated.

"I must obey you without question."

"Excellent. You learn well. Now sit on this chair."

She sat, not able to stop herself from attempting to cover herself.

Alexandr frowned and leaned over her. "Uncross your

legs, Anna. Your body is to be displayed at all times. It is an essential part of your preparation."

Of course, it was. How could she forget the events of the night before? Bracing herself, she adjusted her legs, and placed her hands demurely on her lap.

Alexandr's generous lips twitched. He turned and tugged on the bell pull. Within seconds Darius and Jamie entered the room and flanked both sides of the chair, their expressions unreadable.

"It seems Anna is having difficulty getting into position for this morning's activities. You may assist her."

"It will be our pleasure, Master," said Jamie. He winked at Anna and moved to one side, while Darius chuckled.

Each young man grasped a leg in their warm hands. Jamie lifted her foot and positioned the leg he held over the side of the chair's padded armrest. Darius did the same on the other side.

"We will use the silk, for now."

Both men produced pieces of material from their pockets and tied her ankles in place, the soft fabric skirting the legs of the chair.

Oh my! Her heart thudded and her breathing quickened. "Please...I am not sure about this."

"It is natural to feel fear at the start Anna. Take a deep breath and let us enjoy viewing your body." He stepped forward and stroked a finger over her exposed folds. She shivered, not knowing why such a debased position made her tingle in pleasure instead of fear.

"Your body is reacting to the preparation already Anna."

Yes, it was, and she was embarrassed, as it appeared she did not have any control over her reactions. It was as she thought this morning. *My body is no longer mine.* Her face burned as Alexandr placed his finger to his mouth and sucked.

"Your essence is delicious Anna; you should not be ashamed. It is natural to be aroused when your body is admired."

"I have never..."

He held up his hand. "That is why you are here Anna. To have these feelings released. To be *Awakened*. Your first task is to stay in this chair and be silent no matter what happens in this room. Do you remember the first rule?"

She nodded again. "I must obey you, Master."

"Correct. And what command did I give?"

"I am to stay in this chair and be silent."

"Excellent. If you comply you will gain much pleasure." Alexandr moved towards her and held a piece of cloth in front of her eyes. "There is, however, just one more thing before I return to my work."

Before she had a chance to protest, the cloth was tied over her eyes and the room went black. She shook her head in an effort to free herself. "What are you doing?"

"Do not fight it, Anna. The mask will enhance your reactions. Try it for a short while, and if you are still uncomfortable you have the choice to leave. Is that what you wish?"

Did she want to end this? She had already gone further than she had ever imagined she would, and no harm had come to her. She wanted to experience it all. She would not give up yet. "No, Master. I do not wish to leave."

"Excellent. We will continue then."

With her senses heightened, she heard him walk past the

curtain to his desk. "Tend the fire, Darius. We must ensure our guest does not catch a chill."

"Yes Master," he answered.

"Oh, and Jamie—after you finish, you are owed a reward for your work with our client last week."

"Yes Master?"

"You may have two minutes but remember the rules."

"Oh yes, thank you Master."

She felt the heat from his body between her legs as he approached.

Oh God! He is going to touch me there!

She gasped as his fingers parted her folds. She closed her eyes under the scarf, wanting to know what he was doing, but afraid also, lest she enjoy it more than she was ready to admit. Something wet and warm lapped over her and her eyes shot open. She sucked in a breath when she realized she couldn't see anything but the darkness of the cloth.

Never in her wildest imagination had she expected this. Of course, she knew from reading her forbidden books that men feasted on woman parts, but she had no notion that the pleasure would be so intense, especially when her ability to see was taken away. Jamie licked up and down as a tension built inside her like a coiled spring. She knew she needed more but did not know what she sought. Jamie's thumbs moved together to rub over her skin, and she felt her sensitive nubbin swell and harden beneath his relentless pressure. Her head fell back against the chair, her breath coming in short spurts. The tension was building to some unknown peak but just as soon as it had started, all the touching stopped.

Jamie removed his hands and stood. She heard two sets of feet walking away.

"You are correct, Master. She is delicious."

Anna heard the smile in Alexandr's voice. "She is indeed, but do not forget who she is, young man."

Jamie's voice was solemn. "No, I will not forget, Master."

"Good. You may both leave now. I will call again when I have need of you."

Anna shivered as a small breeze teased across her skin and she jumped slightly at the sound of the door closing. She wondered what else the day would bring.

***

Alexandr continued working at his desk for some time. Although he was unable see Anna through the curtain, he could hear her sighs as the time alone was beginning to wear on her nerves. *Be patient a little while longer my dear*. He smiled to himself. The wait would definitely be worth it. Anna was a delight, and he could see she would make a perfect match for his friend. It was rare to encounter such an adventurous and passionate spirit in one who had lived such a sheltered and lonely life.

He sighed, closing the account book he was pretending to read. Perhaps one day he too would find someone as equally suited to him as it appeared Anna was for Justin. There was a time when he thought he had found that perfect companion, only to be deceived by a calculating witch intent on spending all his money while stringing him along with her lies and broken promises. It would take a miracle to convince him to trust again. Justin was indeed lucky to have found his special woman, and he hoped it would work out for him. He would do everything in his power to make it happen. Helping to prepare Anna for his friend was certainly turning out to be a delightful pleasure.

The soft knock at the door came as planned and he smiled at the sharp intake of breath he heard from the other side of the curtain at the scrape of his chair when he stood.

He walked over to draw the curtain open.

"Anna, my dear," he said.

She lifted her head, her luscious body a picture worthy of a Reubens painting. She attempted to sit, only succeeding in pushing her breasts outward, begging for some attention. He sucked in a breath and moved closer to the chair. Justin had best wed her soon, or someone else would claim her. He cleared his throat, appreciating the allure of her innocence and the sight of her pink tongue moving delicately over her top lip.

"Are you ready for your next session?"

Her voice was barely audible. "What are you going to do?"

"You have forgotten the rules again my dear."

She flushed, her pink nipples puckering at his words. Her head dropped forward. "I'm sorry."

He chuckled. She was born to this, but she had a few more lessons to learn before she would complete her *Awakening*. Grabbing her chin, he lifted her face. "You also forgot the proper form of address. What is it?"

He could sense a hint of resentment behind the thick scent of arousal. Good. He let her go but stayed close to her while he waited for her response.

"I'm sorry—Master!"

"Ah, I see the young girl has spirit. We can deal with that."

Moving closer, he whispered in her ear. "Do not forget the rules my dear. Silence, no matter what happens."

He chuckled and walked to the door, opening it wide.

"Come in my friends. Come and meet my guest."

Anna stiffened, but to her credit, she uttered no sound as the small group moved into the room. The servants were well paid for this service and knew well enough never to divulge any of what occurred at the preparation sessions here at Maitland House or they would face the consequences. Since they all valued their employment, and they seemed to be happy here, it had never been a problem. In fact, they seemed to look forward to very much helping him in this duty.

He saw Justin walk into the room as the last of the servants arrived and he frowned. How would his friend react to this part of the preparation? Perhaps he should let him take part? But no, Justin had been adamant he would allow Anna to experience it all as she would, were he not present.

It was time to begin. Alexandr moved to Anna's side and whispered to her. "Do not be afraid, your face is covered. No one knows who you are." Her shoulders relaxed but he knew her reprieve would not last long. He stood and faced the group.

"Friends, you may begin your inspection."

At her loud intake of breath, he placed his hand on her shoulder. "Hush, you will enjoy this, but if you wish to stop you must tell me now."

She breathed in and out, and time stood still while she hesitated. When Justin started to move towards her, she spoke, her voice husky and ragged. "No, I want to do this. You may proceed."

"You are sure?"

She spoke again, this time her voice stronger. "Yes, I am sure Master. Please commence."

Alexandr hesitated, waiting for a reaction from his friend. Justin nodded and retreated to the back of the room.

"Ladies and gentlemen, you heard the lady. You may begin."

One by one the staff of five filed past Anna. As each one approached, they touched her. The first round activity was to use hands only. The first pair were women, and seemed to prefer touching the skin of her cheek and breast, while the men, with their larger hands and rough skin took turns in pinching her nipples or running their fingers over her hairless crotch. Alexandr watched Anna closely. The scent of her arousal was heady and surrounded them as with each touch her breathing became more and more ragged.

From across the room Justin stared at her exposed body transfixed as a tiny trickle of her enjoyment escaped and glistened over the skin of her upper thighs. It was not the first time they had both been present for the pleasuring of one of Alexandr's female clients, but this was different. Anna wasn't a bored widow or a spinster wanting to experience sex any way they could. This was the woman Justin wanted to marry. Alexandr was very aware of the limits but damned if didn't he want to throw them out of the window. This was an amazing woman and if things had been different, and he didn't have another on his mind, he would want to keep her for himself. Fortunately for Justin, he could never dishonour their friendship no matter how big the temptation, but by God, if Justin ever hurt her, he would kill him. The bond he shared with the women he helped at Maitland House was unbreakable.

The second round started, and this time Alexandr allowed them to use their mouths. Anna's moans were loud as the last of the men sucked on her sensitive nub. Her head twisted from side to side, and she ripped the arms of the chairs so tightly her knuckles turned white. It was James taking his turn again, and he played it to his advantage. The women who came to the house often extolled the skill the young man displayed with his tongue, and it seemed this was true. If he did not stop soon, however, he would go too far. Alexandr directed one of the two men guarding her to remind him of his duty and James stood back after being tapped on the shoulder, looking most satisfied with his work.

"This session is finished my friends. You may all leave, and we thank you for your assistance."

Justin nodded to Alexandr as he followed the procession of hand-picked staff from the room. Alexandr knew how difficult it had been for him not to join in. *But it will be worth the effort it in the end my friend.*

Anna slumped back in the chair, her breathing now slowing. Alexandr removed the blindfold, and the ties around her legs. She swayed on her feet as she stood, so he drew her to him, wrapping his arms around her languid body.

"Are you all right my dear?"

"I am well, Master," she sighed.

"Did you find pleasure?"

She squirmed in his arms and tried to move away. "I did not expect to."

He held her firmly in place. "But you did, in spite of your misgivings."

She stared at his face, her eyes burning with a mixture of

shame and restrained passion. "I must be very wicked," she whispered. "Because I did find pleasure. Very much so."

He laughed. "It is not wicked to enjoy others worshipping your body. It is the natural way of things. You did nothing wrong."

She smiled shyly. "I will try to believe that, but my parents taught me otherwise, and it is very difficult to undo the teachings of my upbringing."

He reached for a cupboard behind the chair and removed a robe, placing it over Anna's shoulders. "You have come a long way in a very short time Anna. You are doing very well. Much better than most who come here. Your *Awakening* will be magnificent. Do not forget that."

"You think so sir?"

He smiled at her upturned face and placed a chaste kiss on her forehead. "I know it for a fact."

The door opened and Cassandra entered.

"Go now with Cassandra. You have learned well today. Have some food and rest and we will begin again tomorrow."

"Is my preparation finished?"

"That will be all for today. You will need your rest for what comes tomorrow. Sleep peacefully my dear."

Cassandra moved forward and took Anna's hand. "You did well little one. Come and we will get you fed and bathed."

Alexandr waited until the two women left the room before striding across the room to the side bar where he poured himself a large brandy. As much as he found Anna's charms attractive, there was another lady entirely who roused of his own desires. No— not quite a lady, but she was as innocent as Anna, and he had no business thinking about her at all.

3

Chapter Three

Justin paced the floor of Alexandr's library, his stomach in a knot. Where the blazes was Alex? He hoped like hell he was not too late to change the arrangements for Anna's training. The past few days had been more difficult than he could ever have imagined. His hunger for Anna had grown, and so had his determination to claim her. Nothing had prepared him for the intense feelings he had felt seeing her exposed and reacting with such passion. He had always known she would be daring, but now he needed to know if she was his perfect partner in every way. The rest of this week was all the time he had to show her what pleasures were to be explored, and to assure himself she could accept him and all his desires.

The door opened and Alexandr walked in. His eyes were rimmed in red, and his clothing dishevelled.

"What troubles you, my friend?" he said, staring as his host staggered into the room. "You look like hell."

Alexandr looked up and snarled. "A small case of over-indulgence with a bottle of brandy. Nothing the hair of the dog could not reverse," he said. He reached over the desk and shook the remnants of a near-empty bottle. "I assume you are here to enquire about the progress of your intended."

Justin thrust a hand through his hair and commenced pacing again. "I have another favour to ask, my friend."

"I believe I am building up quite a cache of favours Justin," he said, as colour began returning to his face.

"You have but to ask and I will repay you Alex."

Alexandr help up his hand. "It is of no consequence, Justin. It amuses me to oblige. Witnessing your discomfiture is quite enough payment for the moment."

"You are enjoying this far too much, Alex."

Alex laughed. "Oh yes, it is a treat to see you so befuddled over a woman. I cannot understand it myself. It seems to cause you all manner of trouble, but if that is what you wish, then who am I to complain?"

Justin snorted. "I'm glad I'm providing you with entertainment, but if I do not become more involved, I fear it will be all for naught."

"What services do you wish of Maitland House?"

"I wish to take over Anna's training."

Alexandr sighed. "Are you quite sure my friend? She may recognize you before you are ready."

"At this stage I do not care. I only know if I allow another man to touch her again, I will kill him."

"She does appear to be a treasure."

"Do not forget Alex that she is *my* treasure."

"You need have no fear on my account Justin. I was merely paying tribute to her many good qualities. She is all yours."

"Excellent. I will introduce her to the dungeon."

"Monsieur de Sade would be very proud of you."

"I doubt very much that de Sade would approve of my adaptation of his works. His fixation with pain and humiliation are not to my liking, but I do agree with his explanation of the power to be obtained from the gift of trust."

"Expecting trust and giving it are not always easy, Justin."

"Oh, believe me my friend, this is something I am very much aware of."

* * *

Anna shivered as she was led down a steep staircase the next morning. The blindfold Darius had firmly tied over her eyes not only robbed her of sight but completely changed her whole perception of her surroundings. She moved one foot at a time, sliding her toes in front of her in an effort to feel where she was heading. The temperature cooled the further she was led down the stairs. At first she thought they were heading for a cellar, but with the length of the staircase she feared they were heading deeper into the cellar. She twisted her shackled wrists together and pulled her bent arms closer to her body, valiantly trying to dampen the trepidation she felt. She knew that she had to but say the word and it would all stop, but even though at this stage that was the last thing she wanted, she couldn't help but fear what was coming.

"Where are you taking me?" she whispered.

"You must keep quiet Anna. You are not permitted to speak during this lesson unless given permission," she heard Cassandra say behind her.

She relaxed slightly at the sound of the woman's voice. "If that is what is required, I apologize"

"It is of no consequence. Darius should have explained before bringing you down here."

Anna felt a tug on the leash attached to her shackles. "I am sorry, Mistress. I was distracted," said the husky voice of the trusted servant. "Miss Anna is a most delightful guest."

"Darius! You forget yourself," said Cassandra, her voice stern.

Anna heard a soft chuckle. "Do not worry Mistress. I know what is required. It won't happen again."

"See that it doesn't," said Cassandra.

Anna released a breath and relaxed. She trusted Cassandra would not lead her into anything dangerous. She decided to wait and see what was in store for her before panicking. Her visit to Maitland House had so far been very educational. In fact, it had been the most enlightening experience of her life. She gloried in discovering the feelings she had been experiencing for so many years were not an abomination, but a natural and beautiful thing. In this place she was able to experience all she had dreamed of and more, with the knowledge her secrets would not be shared.

Well, she thought, *almost* all that she dreamed of. Closing her eyes beneath the mask, she thought again of the boy who now was a man grown, most likely with a wife and a brood of children. Would she ever rid herself of his image? Would any other man suffice? In her dreams it was *his* hands she imagined touching her. *His* fingers stroking her most female parts. *His* mouth suckling on her breasts.

Darius stopped walking and placed his hand on her shoulder.

"Be still, we have arrived."

Her heart leapt and her breathing rate increased. "Arrived where?"

"Silence." said a voice she had not heard before. He did not speak loudly, there was no need. His tone defied her to disobey. She did not dare.

She felt the heat of his body as he took a step closer to her.

"Did you not apprise this wench of the rules?"

"Please accept our humble apologies Master J. Apparently Miss Anna did not understand our instructions," said Cassandra.

"Do not blame them," said Anna, she whispered. She did not wish to be the cause of trouble for her protectors. "I was aware of the rules, however I am not used to being tied and blindfolded thus. I forgot myself for a few moments."

"You are to be commended for taking responsibility, so I will let this transgression go," the voice said. "Do not, however, break this rule again."

She felt heat shift in front of her as the body that belonged to the voice moved closer. A hand touched her face, stroking a calloused finger over her quivering lips.

"Next time you will feel the consequences," he whispered against her ear, his warm breath sending tingles across her skin. "You may answer me. Do you understand? "

"Yes," she whispered. Her mouth felt so dry her tongue refused to work and she could barely speak.

His firm hand pinched her chin and tilted her face upwards. "Yes?"

Oh God, I have transgressed again.

"Yes Master. Please accept my very humble apology. I fear I am still learning what is required of me."

She heard a low chuckle above her head, and she was taken back to her childhood, laughing while running through the fields with her best friend the boy she longed for. She blinked under the mask, valiantly trying to bring herself back to the present and what she was about to experience. "Indeed. You are an errant pupil, but I will enjoy teaching you the error of your ways. Come forward little rebel and enter my dungeon for your first lesson."

Wench? Dungeon? All manner of visions instantly flashed across her mind at his words. Instead of being frightened for her life however, she felt the now familiar tingling of heat. The lessons of the previous day had prepared her for a stranger's touch. Although she should be appalled at the thought of restraint and punishment, she thought of the drawings she had discovered in her secret books. The women in those pictures did not act as one normally did when subjected to punitive discipline. On the contrary, their faces portrayed a number of emotions including joy, happiness, and rapture, which until this week she had not been able to define. Now, however, after the previous day's activities, she believed it to be intense sexual satisfaction.

"Move wench!" he chided as he grabbed her wrists and pulled her forward. A heavy door closed behind her, and she turned towards the sound.

"Darius and Cassandra have gone. They are no longer required," he said. "You and I are now totally alone."

She stiffened, wondering if perhaps she should exercise

her right to leave now, before she dropped completely into the well and the unknown.

Anna ran her tongue across her dry lips, unsure what was expected of her beyond the obedience of which she had already been informed. *Who is this man and why does he seem familiar?* Was it his voice? Or the manner in which he spoke? Or was it the feeling she experienced when he touched her face?

He placed a hand between her shoulder blades and ushered her inside. His warm breath whispered across the bare skin of her neck and her heart beat was so loud she was certain he must hear it. Although she had seen drawings of this very situation, nothing had prepared her for the tight knot in her stomach, or the dampness at the juncture of her thighs betraying her arousal.

"Kneel," he said.

She hesitated, not sure if she could negotiate the process without falling. The silence that greeted her was loaded with tension, so she bowed her head and bent her knees, keeping her toes on the floor to steady her descent. The muscles in her calves clenched in pain and she stumbled, desperate to use her hands, but unable to do so due to the tight binding. Her heart leapt into her throat. She felt herself falling, only to be caught by a strong grip on her shoulders guiding her to her knees.

"Thank you."

"It is my duty to care for you. Did you think I would let you be hurt?"

She blinked inside the mask. "I'm...I'm not sure."

"You must learn to trust if we are to complete this part of your experience. Do you think you can trust me?"

"Yes, yes I do," she answered, surprised she had spoken without thinking.

A loud sigh was the only sound she could hear in the stillness of the dungeon.

"Is there a reason I should not trust you?" she asked.

He chuckled again. "You have been here a minute and already you have forgotten the rules twice."

She gasped. "I am sorry..."

He covered her mouth with his warm hand. "Do not say another word. Your transgressions already pile up."

She sucked in a breath as he removed his hand. How could she be so lacking in attention? There was something about this man's voice and this situation that befuddled her. It was not an altogether unpleasant experience either, which if she was thinking at all, she should find more disturbing than she did. But she reminded herself why she was here, and this was something from which she did not wish to run.

There was a sharp tug on the bindings that held her hands, pulling her to her feet. She sucked in some air, more than slightly alarmed at the swiftness of his movements.

"Come with me little rebel. I will place you in your first position to begin our session."

She stumbled forward, led as a blind person by this stranger across the cold room. The cool air chilled her and she shivered, sending goose bumps across her body. He stopped after a few steps and placed his hands on her shoulders, turning her and nudging her backwards. Her skin made contact with a cold surface, and she flinched.

"Do not fear the cold, little rebel. Soon enough you will be feeling the fire of desire."

Before she could form a thought, he placed her arms above her head and fastened them to something metallic jingled above her head. She held her breath, awaiting his next move.

The ties binding her wrists were wrenched higher as the device above her drew her farther from the floor.

She bit her lip to prevent the cry that threatened to escape. She didn't wish to disobey any more than she already had done thus far.

"That is excellent little one. Very good control. We may make some progress this day."

She smiled and her heart fluttered. Despite the discomfort of this position, his words lifted her.

She heard his confident steps walking across the room. He returned to her side, and the heat from his body warmed her. Or maybe it was her excitement? Perhaps it was both.

Judging from the feel of his ragged breathing against her forehead, he was standing right in front of her. The muscles in her upper arms twitched and she stood on her toes to ease the strain.

"You look exquisite like that my dear, all tied up for my pleasure. You may speak if you wish."

She ran the tip of her tongue over her dry lips. "May my arms be lowered Master?"

"No."

"Oh," she gasped.

He chuckled. "I said you may speak. I did not say I would do as you ask of me."

Will I ever understand this game? "My apologies again, Sir. I am new to this house."

He grabbed her chin with a firm hand and moved closer. His hot breath tickled the sensitive skin of her neck. "You have been a guest for two days is that correct?"

"Yes," she whispered.

"You completed the inspection session yesterday?"

She nodded. Her skin heated as she remembered the touch of the staff while she sat fastened to the chair in Master Sakaroff's study.

"You have been here long enough to learn the two rules. I do not see why you continue to break them."

"I..." she began to speak, but he tweaked one of her nipples and twisted it forcefully. She panted, struggling to accustom herself to the mixed sensations of pain, and the growing tingle of arousal. "I... I don't know why I forget."

He replaced his finger with his mouth, sucking deep before nipping the bud with his teeth.

"Aaah..." she groaned.

He stopped the sweet torture. "I think I know," he answered. "You wish to be punished."

"No..."

"Yes," he said, and slapped her across her sex.

She cried out, stunned he would dare touch her in such a way.

He slapped her again, this time catching the side of her breast.

Her nipples grew taut and the tingle in her body deepened and spread to her precious nub. She instinctively rubbed her legs together, but he slapped her thighs.

"You will not pleasure yourself little rebel. That is my prerogative if I so choose to do. And for the moment, I choose not."

"But Master..." she begged.

He laughed. "You cannot help yourself, my wanton one. I will offer you some assistance to keep silent. Once you gain control, I will remove it."

She closed her mouth, shaking her head.

"Open your lips for me, my little rebel."

She gasped, and he slid a finger in, drawing her lips wide. He pushed a soft ball of material between them. She coughed; the taste of the rubbery material was strange. She gasped, worried she would choke.

"Breathe through your nose. There is no need to panic."

She gagged again and tried to expel the ball, but to no avail.

His hand cupped her cheek. "Do not fear it. Breathe. All will be well."

Hot tears trickled down her face, but she reacted to his calming voice and slowed her breathing down, breath by breath. The intensity of her feelings at this moment was immeasurable. *What is happening to me?*

He stroked her hair away from her face and kissed her on the forehead. "That is better. Work through your fear and you will see how it can enhance your pleasure. I know you do not believe me at this moment, but you will, once you experience this way of life, I plan to share with you today."

He stood back and was silent for a few seconds.

"As always, we will not move forward unless you consent to continue. It would disappoint me greatly if you were to choose to end it all now, but that is your choice Anna," he whispered. "Say the word and this all ends, and you can return to your home."

Her heart raced and contemplated what he was saying to her. One part of her was terrified of what was to come, but the other part of her. The part that had spent hours studying drawings of erotic arts. The heart that yearned to experience the extasy she saw in the faces of those women. Those were the parts of her that would not let her give up now.

"Do you wish to continue Anna?" he asked.

She nodded, knowing she was reaching the point of no return, but hoping she would not regret this decision.

She could hear his sharp intake of breath.

"That is good news. Now we will begin in earnest. Do not forget the rules again my lovely lady."

She shook her head. She was determined to experience it all and the intense pleasure Master Alexandr had alluded to.

Her arms sagged while she waited for Master J to commence, now aware all control was out of her hands. It surprised her that she did not rush to leave. Quite the contrary. The fear she felt only enhanced the sensations, and in a strange way she felt freer than she had felt in the days after her parents' death when she realized she no longer had to obey their rules. How was this possible when she was shackled and gagged and unable to fend for herself? She did not know, but she planned to find out.

Master J loosened the device holding her hands. He lowered her arms and removed the ties from her wrists, before massaging the soreness from her arms with his warm hands.

He took her hand and led her somewhere else in the room.

"Come with me and I will find a comfortable position for you to grow used to the ball."

She sucked in a breath, not sure of what he meant.

"Do not fear little one, you will enjoy this position more than the previous one."

She nodded, not quite understanding, but she knew she could decide at any time to finish this session. All she needed to do was protest and she trusted him to stop if she asked, but she did not want to. At least not yet.

He stopped and steadied her with his hand on her shoulder. "Listen carefully. I want your trust and for you to do whatever I ask of you. Do you understand?"

She nodded.

"Excellent. Kneel on the stand you will find in front of you."

She held her hand out and touched smooth wood and soft leather. She leaned forward and gripped the edge as she lowered herself to the kneeler. Master J placed his hand on the small of her back and eased her upper body forward onto a cushioned ledge, almost like a table.

"Turn your head to the side and let your arms drop," he said.

As she complied, she felt a large belt or strap being placed across her waist. She held her breath as Master J fastened it. When he finished, she shifted her body, but she was held fast.

"Are you well, little rebel? Nod your head if that is so."

She complied. She wasn't uncomfortable and was becoming used to the soft ball in her mouth. That didn't mean she wasn't feeling very exposed with her nakedness on view, and her nether regions within reach of anyone who walked into the dungeon.

He walked away from her again and she heard him open a drawer. The sound of metal clinking on metal piqued her curiosity, but she jumped at the noise of the drawer being closed before he returned to her side.

"As a part of your *Awakening*, it is a requirement that you are penetrated. Before I continue, you should nod to show me you understand and agree."

She gasped. Of course, she knew that would be the final consequence of her experience, but she had not thought it would be part of the preparation.

"This is not the final sexual intercourse my little rebel. I am merely helping your body become accustomed so that when you reach the climax of your week you will receive the most pleasurable experience possible. Do you agree to allow me to continue?"

She reacted with a heated flush, and she felt the now familiar tingling of sensation forming between her legs. It seemed her body knew more than her mind, so she agreed with his request.

"Then it begins."

He placed something cold and smooth on her cheek and rubbed it back and forth. "This is a dildo. The name means little delight. If you are well-behaved, perhaps you will experience that as well."

She sucked in a breath. His warm hand parted her buttocks and her muscles contracted while he traced a finger over her sex.

"Your cunny is beautiful. You should be very proud."

She did not believe it possible, but her skin heated further, fuelled by his words. But she smiled beneath the gag. No one had called her beautiful since that one time just before her parents had caught her kissing her childhood best friend. *If only he...*

He placed the tip of the dildo at her entrance and rotated it gently over her tight muscles. "The dildo will assist in easing the passage of manhood inside you. I will be as gentle as I can, but it will pinch at times, so do not be alarmed. I will not go further than your body allows."

She nodded but the distraction of a cold foreign object moving inside her most private parts was making it difficult to think.

"Did you know that some doctors believe that the answer to most women's ailments lies in achieving regular paroxysms?"

She moaned.

He continued moving the dildo.

Her body released more moisture the longer he played, which seemed to please him, judging by the constant words of encouragement he offered.

"Personally, I agree that women are more pleasing creatures if cared for and rewarded in this way, but I feel many are not getting what they need from their husbands. Any woman of mine would not have that problem."

She gasped and cried out against the ball gag when he pushed the object inside her in one quick movement. Her muscles clenched against the intrusion. It took a few minutes for her to accustom herself to the sting. She panted and the coughed against the ball while pulling against her restraint.

Master J placed a hand on the middle of her back and

stroked. "Slow down your breathing and try to relax. In a few moments the pain will pass. You must trust me."

She tried, but she could not stop focusing on the intrusion and as the panic rose, so did her struggle against the gag.

He continued slowly stroking her moving along her back and up to her shoulders. "Listen to my voice little rebel. Trust that I will do you no harm. You are a beautiful woman, and you want this. Remember why you have come to Maitland House."

Gradually her fear lessened, and she slowed her breathing. The dildo remained in place, but no longer pinched. She was calmer now, and Master J moved the dildo in place, scraping it around the edges of her entrance, sending tingles straight to her sensitive bud.

"That is so much better my dear. The pain will now subside, and you will begin to see what can be."

He began rubbing his finger in circles across her bud, while twisting the dildo in a circular motion with his other hand.

"I can see how your body is responding to me. You are everything I ever thought you would be."

She heard his words, but as her breathing rate increased, the pressure inside her was building to something she had never thought possible. It was raw desire, but if something didn't give soon, she was sure she would faint.

"You must let go of your fears, my little rebel. Allow the pleasure to overtake you. Do not fight what your body craves with thoughts of your old life."

She screwed her eyes tight as the face of her childhood friend loomed in her mind. The face of her dreams smiled at her, and she let go. Her legs braced and a flood of pleasure took over as her body contracted around the dildo. It was minutes later when the paroxysms slowed, and she collapsed boneless against the stand.

His warm breath tickled against her ear.

"A woman's pleasure is a beautiful thing my little rebel. I am very proud of you," he whispered.

As she regained her sense of her surroundings, Master J removed the belt from her waist and helped her to stand. He untied the gag and using a soft cloth he wiped the drool off her face but left the blindfold intact. His large body engulfed her in his warmth, and he stroked her back. "You have done very well Anna. Go now and rest. Your lessons have just begun."

She felt someone take her hand as Master J released her. "Come with me Anna."

Cassandra? Where had she come from?

"Thank you, Cassandra. Punctual as always. Our little rebel will be tired. Please ensure she is well-rested and prepared for the next session."

"Most certainly Master J," she answered as she placed a soft robe around Anna's shoulders.

"And Cassandra?"

"Yes, milord?"

"Remind the assistants who this lovely creature is."

"Of course."

His warm lips touched Anna's forehead and she shivered.

"Rest well my little rebel. I look forward to our next adventure."

4

Chapter Four

Anna tossed and turned as sleep eluded her. She'd returned to her room in a daze. When she'd arranged to come to Maitland House, she had known what she'd wanted. To be taken by a man. To experience an *Awakening*. She was most definitely being awakened. She realized she'd been naive to believe she'd known what she would find there. In two short days she'd discovered more about pleasure than she'd imagined. Alexandr Sokoloff had promised her this would be the case and he certainly had not lied. Even with her maidenhood technically intact, she felt more like a woman now than she had ever felt before. She thought back to her session in the dungeon with the enigmatic Master J. Her body heated as she relived every touch, every reaction. But it was much more than the way he touched her that captured her imagination. When she closed her eyes she saw her childhood friend, but he was not the same boy he'd been when she'd last seen him.

He was now a man, and in her dreams, he still wanted her, even though she knew this was nigh impossible. *But oh, how I wish it could be him.* Perhaps that was why Master J affected her so. Although a perfect stranger to her, he touched her as if he cared, and his voice with its deep timbre sent tingles across her skin with every word while dominating her—even while she stood helpless to repel his advances. But she did not fear him. At no time did she feel the need to escape, even though she knew if she spoke the words, it would all finish. That was not a choice she had made thus far. She wanted it all to continue.

What manner of woman am I to feel pleasure in being restrained and touched by a man?

Did it really matter? It wasn't likely she would marry given her spinster status and lack of fortune. Her parents had been quite successful at destroying her chances at happiness when they had separated her from her soul mate. They'd believed he was beneath their status, but in truth, he had more integrity in his little finger than any of the procession of weak-willed males her father had thrown in her path over the years. Once her parents had become ill, she'd withdrawn from society completely. Her only escape had been the fantasies she found in the forbidden books. They had sustained her through the difficult times when her parents had displayed such a level of paranoia that she dared not leave her room, lest they find fault and lock her in the tower room. The few times she had escaped the house to spend time with school friends had taught her they meant what they said. She was no more than an hour away when their staff had found her and brought her back to the virtual prison, she had lived in for most of her life.

But that life was behind her. Now she could go where she pleased and do as she wished. But the habits of a lifetime were difficult to break. It was only this past day with Master J she had felt it possible to be free of her past. Being uninhibited enough to entrust her body to another was one thing—but to feel such pleasure left her with a totally unexpected feeling of peace. She hoped this would sustain her when her time here was at an end. She planned to travel and enjoy her independence, and this experience was her first step to gaining back the self-confidence of her youth. As she blew out the lamp she smiled. There would be no regrets. Only pleasurable memories.

She gasped as the quilt covering her naked body was thrown back.

"What is happening," she whispered. With no candle alight, the room was so dark she couldn't see.

Her wrists were grasped firmly, and she was pulled into a sitting position before a soft material was tied around first one, then the other hand.

"Do not fear my love," said a voice in her ear.

She relaxed when she recognized the voice of Master J.

He guided her to stand, and she shivered at the chill in the air. "I was under the impression the next lesson wasn't until the morning sir."

"I changed my mind. We are continuing on from our session this afternoon, which means you must continue to follow the rules. Do you remember what that means?

"Yes Master J."

"Tell me, so I can assure myself that you will behave in the correct manner."

"My body is yours to do with as you please."

"That is correct. What else do you remember?"

"I must only speak when given permission."

He lifted her hands to his mouth and kissed her on both palms. "I am pleased little one. You have learned much in a short time."

His words warmed her and sent a tingle across her skin.

"What is it you wish of me Sir?"

Although it was dark in the room, she could feel his eyes boring into hers. She'd broken the rules already. This was going to be interesting.

"My apologies Master J. I spoke without permission. I am not very good at these lessons."

She heard him release a breath and laugh. "I will allow this one transgression since you apologized so nicely. But watch out as I may not be as generous next time."

"Thank you, sir."

He placed a finger over her lips. "Hush now, or you will find out what I meant."

She nodded, her heart beating fast. She reminded herself she was safe here and the reward would be worth it if she cooperated with her teacher.

"Good. I can see you are ready to continue. Please follow me and together we will experience pleasure above and beyond what you could ever imagine. Nod if this is what you want."

Oh yes. She nodded without delay, not wanting him to have any doubts.

"Excellent," he said.

He walked towards the door, but she struggled to follow him in the darkness, praying she wouldn't fall. As they continued to the end of the hallway, she hoped to catch a glimpse of his face—a face she had yet to see, but alas his face was covered with a domino mask, adding to the air of mystery surrounding him. He passed the last door and before he alighted the stairs he turned and took her arm guiding her down the steps so she would not fall. At the first landing he released her arm and took the lead again. Her eyes were now more used to the darkness, and she could just make out the ornateness of the furnishings. No doubt this floor was for the wealthier clientele, but she was more than happy with her own rooms. Halfway along this level they came to a set of heavy double doors. Before they reached them the doors opened and she saw inside.

Dozens of candles lit the space and two servants, one male and one female, stood to the side of a large four-poster bed. Master J walked into the middle of the room and turned to face her. She took his cue and stood silently, blushing furiously as she remembered she was naked and standing in front of three strangers.

"Isn't she lovely?" he said.

"She is indeed most beautiful," said the maid.

"You are most fortunate to have her in your care, Master," said the male servant she did not recognise.

"Yes. I am indeed. Have you completed the arrangements?"

"Yes, Master J," said the maid.

He nodded. "You may leave."

They both bowed before leaving the room.

Anna jumped as the heavy doors closed behind them. What did he have planned for her?

"Close your eyes."

She obeyed, shivering despite the warmth from the fire.

"Good. Do not open them until I tell you to. Did you find during your first session with Master Alexandr that removing the sense of sight enhances the pleasure? You may answer."

She gulped, her nipples tightened and her whole body tingled at the memory of that first day. "Yes Master."

"So, you found it pleasurable to have strangers touch your body outside of your control?"

She nodded again.

"You may speak. Tell me what you felt."

Her mouth felt dry, and her heart pounded. "I...I don't know what you mean Sir."

"Tell me about the pleasure you felt."

She squeezed her eyes shut tighter, struggling to find the words for something so new in her realm of experience. "It is difficult for me Sir. What I experienced was wicked."

"So, you think you have done wrong?"

"No! I mean—in my past this would have been the case, but now I do not care if it is wicked or not."

He laughed. A deep laugh that made her heart skip a beat. "I am glad to hear that, Anna. I would hate to be accused of corrupting you."

She giggled. "I am here of my own volition Sir. If anything, I am corrupting *you* by seeking this service."

This time he took her face in his hands and kissed her soundly on the mouth. "You are everything I knew you would be and more."

Before she had time to ponder on his words, he was leading her across the room. He turned her around and then pushed her gently onto the bed. She slid over the soft silky sheets as he positioned her body to lie in the middle of the mattress.

"I will be restraining you again little rebel. Tell me now if you don't wish to do this. If you are silent, I will continue."

She smiled. Of course, she wanted this. Her body and her spirit craved it already and it was only a few hours since she had met this man.

"Hmm. I believe your silence is giving me permission to finish this," he said.

The touch of his hands on her skin as he removed the ties on her wrists warmed her

"As before, my love, your body is mine to do with as I please. You can be assured your maidenhood will remain intact until the appointed time, but there will be more preparation taking place this night."

At this moment in time, she didn't care if he wished to claim her prior to her last evening here. It seemed impossible to her that she would last another five days until then, but she did not want to miss any of the delights they had planned for her, and to pre-empt that would be to cheat herself. This was not the reason she had decided to come here in the first place, and she wasn't about to change her mind at this late stage of the process.

She sighed as his warm mouth sucked on her taut nipple.

He raised her arms above her head. "Your skin is so soft, like rose petals."

His hot breath blew over her nipple and her body arched to meet him, begging for more.

"Do not worry my love. We have all night for this. After

our time in the dungeon, I have been thinking of a hundred and one ways to tease you while you are under my tutelage."

His words sent her mind into a whirl. She couldn't imagine anything more decadent than what he was already doing.

She tensed as he took one hand and stretched it towards one of the posts and she heard a click as a something cold encased her wrist.

"Do not be afraid my little rebel—the metal rings are not tight and will assist you to stay in place."

He did the same with her other hand before moving to her feet and spreading her legs apart to secure them in a similar manner.

She struggled against the metal rings She felt so exposed.

"Do not be embarrassed, Anna. Your body is beautiful as many have already told you. It is my pleasure to look upon you. It is my right as your Master."

He stroked a soft trail along her skin from her navel to the top of her folds.

Oh, my goodness. She tried very hard to keep quiet, as Master J had instructed her to, but she could not help letting out a groan. The sensations he was eliciting from her took all control away from her reactions.

Master J chuckled. "Your body is responding to me just as I have planned. Do not fight it and the pleasure will be heightened."

His finger continued its trail, sliding back and forth increasing the tension in a place inside her she had never known existed.

The mattress next to her dipped and he lay beside her, nuzzling her ear and blowing soft breaths against her skin.

Tingles exploded, and she gasped when something cold slid inside her.

"Ah..."

"No no no...there *will* be no talking wench."

She closed her mouth tightly, biting on her top lip to stop the sounds escaping. He was dominating her, but despite this she felt safe, so she pushed her misgivings aside and attempted to let go.

"That is better," he whispered. "But do not relax too much for I have a few more surprises planned for you before this night is over."

He manipulated the cold object, and the feeling of fullness increased. Her body objected, clamping around it but he continued, sliding it further. She whimpered at the strange sensation of being stretched.

"Do not fear little rebel. This will ensure that when the time comes for your final *Awakening* there will be no pain...only pleasure." His voice was smooth as silk. He stroked her cheek to wipe away a tear escaping from her closed eyes. "However, I do not wish to overwhelm you too soon. The past few days must have been confusing and emotionally draining on you. If this is too much you have only to speak up and we will stop."

She shook her head when he stopped what he was doing.

He drew closer to her, and his hot breath brushed across her face. "Does that mean no more? You may speak."

She swallowed and cleared her throat before speaking. "No. Don't stop."

"Don't stop what?"

"Don't stop, Master," she said, her voice croaky. "Thank you for preparing me, Sir."

"Well done my little rebel," he said. "You have taken to this like a duck to water."

She gasped as the tiny nerves surrounding her entrance tingled with a mixture of tiny pin pricks of pain—but the build-up of sensations was as far away from discomfort as she'd ever experienced.

"That's it, my little rebel." His voice purred in her ear and reminded her of the smooth rum her father had forbidden in the house, but she had secretly shared with the servants each Christmas. It burned and soothed at the same time. It reminded her of home and her childhood, and that surprised her. Her sheltered childhood was the furthest from what she currently was experiencing than she could ever get.

The tension built even higher as her body became accustomed to the intrusion. Master J kissed her, starting at her sensitive neck before making his way to the mound of her breast. He took her nipple in his mouth and grazed the tip with his teeth. She sucked in a breath at the exquisite pain and marvelled at the glorious internal connection between her breast and her most private parts. *Surely, I will die of this pleasure?*

"Did you know that our French cousins call the climax Le Petit Mort—the little death?" he whispered.

Did I speak aloud? She panicked, knowing she must have disobeyed. She nodded. She had read of this condition, but until now she had never understood the significance of those words.

Master J did not stop his movement with his toy, and she

stopped all thought as arched off the bed and the tension intensified like the tightening of a spring.

Then it all stopped. The object was swiftly removed, and cool air wafted over her body as the Master left the bed.

"No!'

He laughed. "You do not get to choose when your petit mort happens my little rebel. And for your impertinence, you have earned a small punishment."

"Sir?"

"Even now you forget your place. A punishment is to remind you that your Master's control is for your benefit. You must always obey his commands unless you request a stop to the activity. Do you understand? Nod if you do."

She thought about his words. From her scant knowledge of the writings of de Sade, many of these activities could cause harm if the proper care was not taken, so what he was saying was sensible. However, knowing this and being able to give that level of trust was difficult. Especially when she was undertaking a rebirth of her independence.

"Anna? Do you wish to stop now? If that is the case, you will be taken to your room and tomorrow Master Alexandr will discuss a different program with you. Is that what you want?"

"No!"

He let out a loud sigh, but his voice betrayed a hint of humour. "I am pleased you wish to continue, but again you did not obey the instruction. Perhaps I am expecting too much of you. You may open your eyes."

She did as he asked, opening her eyes and blinked a few times while she grew accustomed to the moonlight. She looked up at his face. Although most of his upper face was covered with a black mask there was something about his eyes that warmed her. Here she lay, naked and tied to the bedposts like an animal about to be slaughtered, but she felt no fear.

"Look at yourself my little rebel."

She reluctantly lowered her head to observe her body.

"Can you see what I see?"

She shook her head. *What is he asking of me?*

"I see a woman who has given me the gift of trust. A woman who is here in my room and allowing me to enjoy her pleasure. To me that is the greatest treasure of all."

She looked again as her body responded to his words. Her nipples were taut, and her skin flushed in the soft candle-light. She had been educated to be believe that to look upon your own body was immoral. Even though she knew that was erroneous thinking, and despite all her book reading, she still felt a twinge of guilt when she examined herself but hearing what Master J said gave her the confidence to let go of some her past learnings.

He opened the metal rings encircling her wrists and ankles, rubbing her skin as he did. "I think this is enough for this night my little rebel. I cannot help myself—I do enjoy teaching you the art of desire; however, I forget your innocence. We will continue tomorrow."

He helped her to stand and kissed her softly before wrapping a quilt around her shoulders. The door opened and the maid returned.

"Please return Anna to her room."

The maid curtseyed. "Yes Master J."

As the maid led her away the Master spoke once again. "I

have not forgotten you still require a punishment, little rebel. Think well on what I have said so you may be better prepared when we next meet."

She turned her head to face him and nodded before the maid led her out of the room and closed the door.

* * *

Justin slumped down on the bed and removed his mask. *My God, how am I going to endure until the end of the week?* Anna was more than he had ever imagined she would be, and he knew with a little prompting he could take her sooner than planned, but that would ruin the experience she so desperately wanted. The *Awakening* she had been so willing to risk her reputation and future on, should her attendance here ever be become public knowledge. He wasn't about to ruin her plans, although he hoped she would forgive him his own part in them. Even now he feared she would recognize him at any time and if he did not get the chance to explain to her, she may not wish to see him again. He would not accept that outcome.

She would be his as she was always meant to be.

Perhaps he should have allowed Alex to continue the preparation, but after that one session he witnessed, the thought of another man touching her was like daggers to his heart. It had taken him years to find her again, although he had always known where she was. He had believed her parents when they had told him he would never be her husband so, he had walked out of her life thinking he was doing the right thing. Now he had a second chance, and he wasn't about to ruin it by losing control of his emotions. His years on the continent learning the delicate nuances of this type of relationship had taught him that to be the dominant partner he had to be always in control, and this evening had shown him how difficult it was where Anna was concerned. He had cut the evening short more for his own benefit than for Anna's if he was to be entirely truthful.

He lay on the bed and ran his fingers through his hair. Perhaps it was time to step back and return to the plans he and Alex had originally discussed. His error had been his eagerness to spend time with her, but he had to remember the prize at the end, and to sacrifice that for a moment's pleasure was unthinkable.

But she was so beautiful, this strong and vulnerable woman, and he was so happy to see that her years with those monsters who called themselves her parents, had not changed her heart nor killed her spirit. She appeared to be the same caring and adventurous spirit he remembered. The same as the day he'd fallen in love with her so long ago.

A knock on the door interrupted his thoughts. "Come in."

A dishevelled Alexandr walked in, smiling at him with a bleary-eyed grin as he staggered into the room.

"What's got you in such a fine humour Alex?"

"Oh, I just love it when plans come to fruition."

"Of what plans to you speak?"

"Nothing I can speak of just yet, but it concerns the lovely Cassandra."

"Good. I'm in the mood for some good news."

Alexandr laughed. "All in good time my friend. So, what has you scowling my friend? Does it not go well with your childhood love?"

"It is going too well. I need to step back."

"You want me to take her back on?"

"No! I just need to slow down and not overwhelm her. This place is foreign to her."

Alexandr placed two glasses and a bottle of port on the small desk at the side of the room. "Do not worry my friend. I am sure you will work out the best way to woo her. You know her better than any of us here I suspect."

"Yes, this is true. And it is because I know her well that I fear she may not like the surprise I have planned for her. She may not want to see me again—who knows what poison against me her parents planted in her mind."

Alex poured them both a drink and handed Justin a glass. "She does not seem to me to be the type of girl to believe falsehoods. She is a beautiful woman with a beautiful heart. I can see that myself from the short time I have spent with her. Totally guileless."

"I believe that too, but still, I have my doubts. I need to tread carefully, or I will spoil all my plans."

"I have faith in you, my friend. You need to trust your instincts. That is the basis of our life choices is it not? Trust? Does she not trust you already?"

Justin took a sip of the amber fluid, before placing the glass back on the table. "She appears to, but my fear is that once she realizes who has been preparing her and who is planned for her *Awakening*, she will believe I tricked her, and then any trust I have gained will be gone forever."

"Then tell her now my friend. Get it over with so you can move on."

"Therein lies my dilemma. If she repulses me and insists on

another Master, I will surely kill him before I allow anyone else touch her."

"But surely the choice will be hers. She is here to assert her independence—she told me herself in her letter of application. If you give her back that choice, she will be more likely to forgive."

Justin nodded. "I see your point, but I do not know if I want to take that chance."

"You think if you seduce her then she will be so enamoured she will want to continue after this week."

"That is my current plan, but I am increasingly worried it will backfire. She was always the most open person I knew. Subterfuge is not something she is likely to tolerate."

"Did she care for you once?"

"I believe she did."

"Then you need to trust her as well as yourself. If she cared for you once, she will care for you again once you have told her the truth."

"I hope you are right my friend."

"Didn't I tell you? I am always right!"

Justin laughed as he walked his friend to the door.

"You are also intoxicated and need to retire for the evening."

"You sir—are no fun."

"My apologies but as you say I have much to think about. I will speak to you in the morning with my decision."

"Excellent. I know you will make the correct one. Just like mine with Cassandra. I've decided she needs a man of her own."

Justin smiled. "I wish I had your optimism, but I think

that like Anna, Cassandra would want to make her own mind up on this."

"Nonsense. The man I have in mind is perfect for her, as she is for him."

"You know she is in love with you Alex."

Alexandr sighed. "I believe she believes that, but it is only gratitude and a great friendship that she feels. Once she experiences real love, she will know the difference."

"And in the meantime, you can assuage your guilt for not returning her feelings by finding someone to replace you in her affections."

"That's a cold way of looking at it, Justin."

"But true all the same."

"Perhaps. But I have her best interests at heart. If that works out, we will all be happy."

"And what of your happiness Alex?"

Alexandr shook his head. "I will be relieved once all my friends find their true partners. That will make me happy."

"I'm not so sure I believe you."

He laughed. "My greatest love is in making others happy. This is why I started this establishment, as you know."

"If you keep telling yourself that, you will certainly believe it to be so."

"Of course, it is true. I never lie."

It was Justin's turn to laugh. "In that case my friend, I wish your plan every success."

Alex bowed and backed into the corridor. "As I do yours." He dipped his head in salute and walked away. "Sweet dreams."

Sweet dreams indeed. Justin returned to his bed to think

about all that had happened these past few days, and to decide what he should do about Anna. He did not expect any sleep at all.

5

Chapter Five

Anna woke slowly, her body relaxed but achy. She smiled. Her twitching muscles reminded her of what her Master had done to her this past night. This adventure she had set herself upon was so much more than she had ever have imagined, and she delighted in the fact there were four more days. But she also realized when the week was at an end, she was not sure she wanted this experience to end.

She had secretly read from the works of M. de Sade whenever she dared. It was within those forbidden pages that many of her fantasies had come to life. It had been difficult hiding her activities given her parents had required her to tend to them day and night as they advanced in years. For ten years she had been a prisoner in her own home. Reading by candlelight while her father slept had been her only escape from the life of subservience that had been her lot. In her mind, she had doubted she would ever be able to give herself over to another and lose all control, but the fantasy she had developed for herself differed somewhat from M. de Sade's descriptions. Her dream lover cherished her, not expecting her to behave as the slave preferred by de Sade. She was finished with being at someone else's beck and call. Caring for her parents had not been a choice.

This was different. Which was why she'd asked for the De Sade experience. Just once she wanted to be the one cared for, but she also knew such control came with conditions. In particular—trust. She began to realise—with trust came freedom, however in the back of her mind a small part of her still believed she was being wicked. Sinful. Master Alexandr had reassured her nothing that gave pleasure could be bad. In her heart she knew this to be true. Especially for herself, as the one experiencing it, and no one else was being hurt. But *she* could be hurt, and that worried her the most. Not physically. She knew she was safe here, and that no one would do anything to her she did not want or desire, but what if she could not stop the growing emotional attachment she had for Master J? And worse, what if it became common knowledge that she had attended this place? She cared naught for her own reputation, but a scandal would hurt her loyal servants and she would never wish for that. They were the only family she had left in the world, and she would protect them with her life

She closed her eyes and sighed. The twinges in her muscles brought her back to the present, and to her experience of the past three days, which served to strengthen her resolve. This was her *only* chance to fulfil her dream and she did *not* intend to ruin it. Not when she'd come this far. The liberties she had allowed with her body since arriving in Maitland House astounded her. But the feelings they evoked were the most confusing thing. She had always been curious to know more of the sensual acts, but nothing had prepared her for this intensity.

And what of Master J? He felt so familiar. Comfortable. And very personal. Unlike her interactions with the other staff here at Maitland House, which although they were wickedly arousing and enjoyable, she was very aware these people were performing a service. A service she had paid them well to provide. With Master J however, she felt cared for, and it was enticing, addictive and very dangerous to her psyche. She could feel herself becoming more attached each time they were together, but she knew her stay was temporary. Should she hold back or request another trainer? Or should she allow herself this one indulgence before she returned to her solitary life? She knew the answer before the question formed in her mind. She had started this journey, and she would finish it.

She lay back against the luxurious bedding and silk pillows and stretched her arms above her head, enjoying the textures and luxury of not needing to hurry to be anywhere. *I could get used to this.*

A clock chimed somewhere in the house, and she counted the bells. midday already? *What extravagance this is.* She threw back the bedclothes and sat up, her legs dangling over the side of the enormous bed. It took her a few moments to realise that the fire in her room had already been lit, and a tray of delicacies had been placed on the table in front of the hearth. She jumped up in delight and took a sip of the steaming hot chocolate just as the door to her room opened.

She scrambled to grab the peignoir draped across the chaise longue at the foot of her bed but even with holding the garment close to her body it did nothing to hide her nakedness.

"Drop the clothing little rebel."

She did as commanded but could not bring herself to lift her head and meet the gaze of this man who had given her so much pleasure over the previous day.

"In this house you wear clothing only at our choosing. I choose that you do not. What have you to say to that? You may speak."

She shuffled her feet, not knowing what was expected of her other than to allow him to do as he pleased with her, unless she said the word. Then it would all stop, and she did not wish that. She risked a glance in his direction, hoping the mask would not be in place so she could see his face, but alas the black domino remained. So, she said the only thing she could say to continue. "I am very sorry Master J. I should not have reached for the gown, but in my defence, I believe it will take more than three days to undo the confines of my upbringing. That being said, I offer my sincerest apology."

He strode towards her, and her heart leapt. She waited for what would happen next, but he stopped in front of her, close enough for her to inhale the musky scent that was his alone.

She waited, but all she could hear was his breathing. She held her own, not sure what he expected of her. She was determined to follow the rules as much as she could, trying to be patient and trust him, although it was difficult. She had to restrain a giggle when she thought about what her old governess would say if she saw her now. Not the nakedness, for that would surely have given her apoplexy, but the effort she was making to obey. As a child it had never been a strength of hers.

"You find this amusing Anna?"

She shook her head, hoping she had not ruined things already.

However, there was a smile in his voice when he touched her chin and tilted her face to look at him. "I trust you were thinking pleasant thoughts. You may answer."

"I was thinking of how hard I am trying to obey the rules, and it reminded me of my childhood."

His eyes narrowed. "You enjoyed the restrictions of your childhood?"

"Not particularly sir. It was more that I was not very good at them."

"Then what was amusing to you just now."

She turned away as the heat of a blush filled her face. "I was thinking of my old governess."

"And that made you smile? You must have a great affection for her."

"Actually no. I could not stand her."

"Then I'm not sure why you were smiling."

She laughed now. It was an unlikely position she was in, standing here as naked as the day she was born in a room with a stranger she'd only met the day before. A stranger who she was allowing to command her, and here she was enjoying a silly conversation with him.

"You do not think I meant for you to answer me?"

His eyes sparkled so she wasn't yet concerned until she

heard his next words. She could hear her heart hammering in her chest. Surely, she had not transgressed by smiling?

"You are mistaken little rebel." You will pay for your impertinence."

"I was merely thinking of how my life is so different now, and that my strict governess would be turning in her grave to see me trying so hard to follow rules."

His lips twitched ever so slightly, and she relaxed. Perhaps he understood her after all.

"You should have explained that in the first instance instead of me having to drag it out of you. Remember that as your Master here at Maitland House I am responsible for your welfare. This includes caring for your emotions as well as your physical wellbeing. You may not know the reason behind the question, but you are to trust me that I know what I am doing."

She lowered her head, not quite sure she understood, and wondering if this was something she could get used too. Having to account for every thought and action was a condition she had experienced with her parents, and it wasn't something she wanted to continue. Although what he described was somewhat different in intent. Her parents wanted to control all of her life, but he wanted to care for her.

"Forgive me sir, but I am not in the habit of sharing confidences. I spent many years with only my parents and our servants for company."

"I will allow this one offense, but you must try harder Anna. You have much to learn before this week is over."

"I understand. Thank you, Master J."

He nodded, then gestured for her to turn her back. "Place your arms behind your back, little rebel."

She complied, now becoming familiar with the feeling of being confined. He collected her hands in his fist and a soft material was wound around her wrists. "I have one question, if I may, Sir?"

"I will allow it."

She gulped. Perhaps she should not ask but she could not help it. "Do married men and women who love each other live like this?"

He sucked in a breath and stopped what he was doing. "Yes. Although society frowns on such, and erroneously believes it to be indecent or cruel. However, for many this is the epitome of love. Sharing trust and caring is paramount in any association, but this life takes it to more higher levels than conventional relationships."

Now that she'd started this line of thought she needed to know one more thing. "Have you ever shared this type of relationship with someone you love?" She wondered if she had overstepped, but at the same time did not worry for any consequences of such an erroneous act, as during the course of this conversation, the answer to this question had become very important to her.

He finished tying the soft material around her wrists and gently released his hold on her hands before guiding her to turn towards him. The expression in his eyes through the mask was unreadable, but his lips were tight.

"I have."

She gasped. Just those two words made her heart stop. "So why are you here at Maitland House with me?"

She whispered the question so softly she was unsure if he had heard her, and she wasn't truly convinced she wanted to know the answer but found herself unable to let the subject go.

There was silence for a time, and she thought he was going to ignore her, but finally he spoke, his voice so quiet she barely heard him until he sighed.

"It is complicated."

Now she had opened that box, there seemed to be no way she could close it. "She does not share the same feelings with you?"

He strode purposely to the door. "It is of no concern of yours. I am here. You are here. We have work to do, so follow me to your next session."

She recognised a dismissal when she heard it. The discussion was over, but she was curious about a woman who would not appreciate the care and attention of a man such as Master J. "As you wish, Master J."

As he led the way out of the room, he called out to her. "You must walk two steps behind me and may I remind you to speak only when permitted."

She nodded in response, but he had already moved on. Obedience was expected and she would not disappoint him. Not like that other woman had.

* * *

He was a coward. *A pitiful excuse for a human being.*

The perfect opportunity to be honest with Anna and admit who he was had dropped into his lap and he'd walked away from it. As he led her to the dining area, he thought of how Alex would chide him for not taking his advice. Perhaps he was right, but he had to believe she would prefer to complete her week first, as she had endured a lifetime where she'd had little choice but to fall in with her parents' directives. This experience would give her the opportunity to choose something for herself for the first time since she had been that wild, spirited creature he'd gotten to know and love, and he did not want to be the one to steal that away from her. He had no doubt should she find out his identity now, she would leave before the week was out. And he couldn't do that to her. She wanted this for herself, and *damn*, he wanted it for her as well, as long as *he* was the one to give it to her.

But he also knew the longer she was in the dark about his identity, the more she would feel betrayed. When he'd first concocted this plan, he'd believed he could seduce her enough that she would forgive him the subterfuge. Now he wasn't so sure. Life had not been kind to her, and she deserved honesty.

If only he knew if she still had memories of him. *Does she still dream of me as I do her? Does she remember our first magical kiss?* He'd made a solemn promise to himself that he would not take her fully until she knew the truth, and he owed her that much. And if she didn't forgive him, so be it. But how he prayed she would. All this preparation would not be for naught.

The sound of laughing in the distance reminded him of the event he had planned. This particular activity was always a favourite among the guests, and he hoped Anna would find pleasure in it. It was certainly the most hedonistic party at Maitland House, and he was glad Alex had agreed to arrange it to occur this week during Anna's visit. If any session would prove that she would fit into this life—the life he wanted to share with her, then this was it. But his stomach churned with the fear of her rejection once he revealed himself to her.

As he approached the dining room door he hesitated. He turned to Anna before entering. Her head was lowered, but she stopped in place, as expected. She had taken to his instruction with more speed than he could ever have imagined, and the grace with which she stood belied the fact she was naked and bound, and soon to be in the presence of many others who would see her completely and in all her glory. If it were not for the small twitch of her smallest toes on the carpet underneath her bare feet, he would not have detected any nerves at all. She must hear the din coming from the room, but had not run the other way, nor sought to escape, which she could do at any time. He was so proud of her he could burst, and he knew there were men in this room who would want her for their own, but tonight was not the time for her to choose. He knew there was always a possibility she would reject him in favour of another and this in part was his reasoning for this night. She needed to know there would be choices she could make. The power was within her heart, and he wanted her to be happy. If she did not desire such a life with himself, he would make sure she found what she deserved with someone he trusted.

The door opened and the noise of the revellers inside increased. He heard Anna's intake of breath and smiled to reassure her. "Are you ready for an adventure my beautiful little rebel?"

She looked up at him. He saw a flicker of uncertainty in her face before she straightened her shoulders and blew out a whisper of air. "An adventure is what I seek in this place,

Master J. It is the reason I am here, but I find that each day the butterflies of anticipation increase."

He narrowed his eyes and touched the delicate skin of her face before tilting her chin. "Do you wish to stop? You are always in control here. If this is too much, we will cease everything."

Her breathing quickened and he continued to caress her face and felt the beat of her pulse jump. He held his breath waiting for her response.

"No!"

He laughed in relief. *Thank the Lord!* "Are you sure? No one will think less of you."

She shook her head. "I'm sure."

He started to speak, but she continued.

"My apologies if I misspoke," She bowed her head. "I am very sure Master. I would always wonder if I did not finish what I have started. This will be my only opportunity to experience such things. Once I return to my life, I shall be my old self again."

His relief was palpable, but he dared not show her his feelings until she had received all that she had requested from her time here, and that didn't include an emotional attachment at this stage. She wanted to experience the freedom of submission, and to ensure she knew exactly what that entailed he would hold his tongue, but he needed to speak to her soon. *Perhaps tonight after this session.*

He turned from her and entered the room "Very well," he said, trusting she would follow.

As they arrived, he saw Alexandr, and Cassandra had prepared the room as per his specific requests. The small group of guests were among his dearest friends, and many had brought their wives with them. He hoped Anna would feel more comfortable with his plans once she realised that her experiences did not need to end once her week was over. Despite what their monarch believed, there were many, many couples who indulged in the same proclivities, and he hoped Anna would crave it once she had the taste for it.

As Anna entered behind him, her head bowed as instructed, he looked around at his friends and smiled. The admiration in their eyes made him proud to think that this woman could be his. Of course, he still had no guarantees but if it was at all within his power, she would belong to no one else.

Two servants moved to her side and halted her progress. She looked up hesitantly and searched for his presence. He nodded at her, hoping to reassure her that all was well. She appeared to relax and lowered her head once more before being ushered to a large table in the middle of the room. One of the servants held her hand and guided her onto a step to the top of the table and helped her to lie down face up. She shivered as she lay on the cold wood, but Justin wasn't concerned as the fireplaces had been lit as per his instructions. And given the activities that were about to begin she would soon heat up.

Alexandr approached the table. "She has made excellent progress under your tutelage Master J," he said. "You should be very proud." Alexandr leaned forward and whispered something into Anna's ear, to which she responded with a slight nod.

Justin had to restrain himself from snatching his friend

away. He knew Alex had a stake in the success of his business, and of course Anna was a paying customer, but in this case it was different. And he fully intended to pay for Anna's time here himself. He could not have his woman being accused of scandal and he would spare her in any way he could.

He heard a discreet cough behind him and realised Alex was waiting for a response. "I am well pleased with my charge."

Alex laughed. "And so is your pupil. She has confirmed that her experience is everything she was hoping it to be. At least up until this minute." He stepped back and away from the table. "We must ensure that the remainder of her stay does not disappoint."

The acrid taste of fear settled in his mouth while he weighed the risks of this session and the consequences of it not going well. He made a decision. He hoped it was the correct one and that Anna would understand.

"I agree. However, I feel a change in pace may be needed." Alexandr cocked a brow as Justin removed the restraints and assisted a confused Anna to stand up.

"This is a surprise my friend."

Justin nodded to him. "I know what I am doing Alex."

Alexandr smiled. "Of course. You have my entire staff at your disposal. Let them know what it is you require."

Justin searched the room until he saw who he was looking for. "Cassandra, I have need of you."

Cassandra crossed the room in an instant, in that quiet, elegant way she had of walking without sound. "What is it you require, sir?"

"Please ensure Anna is clothed appropriately, then bring her back here to the celebration."

Cassandra nodded. "As you wish, sir."

Cassandra took Anna's hand and started to lead her to the door.

"Cassandra?" he said.

Cassandra paused and turned to face him. "Yes sir?"

"Once you leave this room you may also remove the blindfold."

"Of course, sir," she said.

After Cassandra let Anna out of the room Alexandr moved to his side.

"What is the plan my friend?" he asked.

Justin took the glass of scotch offered to him by the serving staff and drank it down in one gulp.

"I don't have one, but I looked around the room and realised that if my future with Anna is to have any success, she should be given more free choice."

"I cannot disagree with you there, but what of her program? Her *Awakening*?"

"If what transpires today is not successful, then you will honour the rest of her wishes and ensure she gets what she has paid you handsomely for."

Alexandr laughed. "This is a bold move, Justin."

"I cannot in good conscience continue to lie to the woman I wish to marry."

"You cannot be faulted for your caution my friend. Many relationships have failed because the men and women were not suited."

"But I find that honesty and integrity mean more to me. And the Anna I grew up with would agree."

"I wish you the best of luck."

"I am hoping that luck will not be needed. I am trusting my heart on this, but I know that if I fail, I will indeed need to walk away. I do not wish to use coercion, only the truth. Anna has lived with lies and deception for too long with her selfish, self-serving parents. She deserves better."

"Yes, but she also merits receiving what she has paid for."

"If I succeed, she will definitely experience all that and more."

"For evermore?"

"Exactly."

* * *

Anna was confused. It appeared to her something happened to change Master J's mind once she entered the room. Perhaps he did not wish to continue to teach her? Was she to be send away before she completed her time here at Maitland House?

"Why are you so sad, Anna? You should be proud. You have made much progress these past few days. You are a beautiful and confident woman, and what you are doing takes much courage."

"I would like to believe that I have this confidence of which you speak, but I am concerned it will be for nought, as I am about to be removed from Maitland House."

"Why do you believe that Anna?"

"Because Master J sent me away."

"He also asked for you to be returned to the parlour once dressed."

"Exactly. This would be the first time since I have been in this house that it is required for me to be clothed."

"There are more things to learn about yourself that are best found while clothed. You must not fret. You have paid for your experience, and the Master will ensure that you get what you came here for. "

"But what if Master J has tired of me and finds me unworthy of his time?"

"I find that very difficult to believe."

"Then why did he send me away?"

"He bade me to return you. He does not want to send you away." Cassandra walked to the ring pull on the wall and gave it a quick tug. "We will do has he has requested, and soon enough you will have the opportunity to find out what he has in store for you."

"Have you seen him do this before Cassandra?"

She shook her head slightly. "I cannot discuss what has occurred in the past. You understand that the privacy of our guests is paramount."

"Of course. I am pleased that you take this so seriously. However, I do not need to know any personal details. Can you at least let me know if he has behaved such before?"

Cassandra drew in a breath and blew it out slowly. "Master J is not a regular teacher here as such. I am not aware of any previous pupils."

Anna gasped. "But I was under the impression he and the Master were well-acquainted?"

Cassandra bowed her head. "I have said too much. I can only say that he has been a frequent visitor here and yes, he and the Master are friends. He has always been very kind and treats all of us with respect."

"But...?"

"That is all I can say."

The door opened and a maid entered. "Yes, ma'am? How can I help?

"Thank you, Gemma. Can you please bring me the blue gown from the new garments that arrived this morning?"

Gemma curtseyed before turning to leave the room. "Yes, most certainly, Lady Cassandra."

Cassandra walked to the large armoire in the corner of the room and opened the oak door. After pulling out one of the drawers, she withdrew a lacy chemise and a matching white satin corset.

"Whilst we wait for the gown to arrive, we shall start dressing. After you have the shift in place, please stand with your arms out to the side so that I may cinch your waist."

Anna complied, deciding that it might be best to wait and see how the rest of the evening would play out. Cassandra was correct. Alexandr Sokolov had a reputation for following through on his promises, so she would try not to worry for the moment. It wasn't as if she had any choice. She could not go to the constabulary, nor the newspapers if she was cheated. That would cause a scandal and be disastrous for all concerned. She jumped and reached out to steady herself on the bed post as Cassandra began to lace the corset from behind.

"Does this dress feel comfortable Anna?"

The high neck of the pale blue satin garment felt strange after so many days without wearing anything more than a silk robe. Anna caught her reflection in the Cheval mirror and turned from side to side, swirling the full skirt to gain a better view.

"It is a beautiful dress, Cassandra. Unlike any I have worn before."

"It is the wearer who makes it so."

Anna felt her cheeks warm at the unexpected compliment. "You are very kind, but we both know that it is the dress. You have chosen well for me. Please ensure that the price of the gown is added to my account."

"Do not put yourself down, Anna. You are a lovely woman and deserve to wear a dress such as this. Master J has ordered you wear it so there is no need for you to pay. You are a very fortunate woman you know. You have what many women crave, but never achieve."

"I do? And what would that be?"

"Why independence of course. You choose to come here to Maitland House and explore your fantasies. Most women do not have that luxury. Stand tall and proud."

The woman in the mirror who she did not recognise as herself, stared back at her with defiance. What Cassandra said was true. She was no longer living with the constraints her parents and society had placed on her. As a woman of modest means, she was now free to act any way that pleased her, and she fully intended to take advantage. But habits of a lifetime were very difficult to shake.

* * *

Justin held his breath until Cassandra returned to the parlour with Anna. As the woman he had loved for half of his lifetime entered the room he imagined her floating in sea of blue silk surrounding her. Her hair had been piled high on her head and curls pinned in place to surround her beautiful face. He had never seen such beauty. He did not deserve her, but he wanted her with his whole being, and was terrified that should he fail, he would lose her forever. However, she deserved to have full consent in decisions that were to affect the rest of her life. Lord knows she had never had the opportunity to decide for herself in her past. He was still amazed she was still the honest, courageous, and caring girl he remembered. With the life she must have endured, that was surely a miracle in itself. Now he hoped for a second miracle. Her acceptance of him and the life he dreamed of with her.

He waited until she stood in front of him before speaking. At Anna's sudden intake of breath at seeing him, he feared she recognised his adult self. He had no doubts who she was when he'd first seen her in Alex's office, but he had also been expecting to see her. Anna believed him to be living on the Continent. He hoped he would have time to convince her of his sincerity, and that she would understand his motives were formed out of love.

If he was truthful, creating words at this precise moment was proving to be one of the most difficult tasks he had ever performed, but a task he delayed by avoiding Anna's eyes for the time being.

"You have my deepest thanks, Cassandra. You have done well in your assignment."

"It was my pleasure, Master J. However, the beauty shines in Anna, so I fear if I had returned her in a sack cloth, the effect would have been no different."

"You do yourself a disservice, Lady Cassandra. Your taste is as always exquisite."

He sucked in a quick breath before turning to Anna and holding his hand out to her. Her fingers felt cool when she hesitantly clasped his, but he ignored the impulse to draw her into his embrace to infuse some warmth. This change in plans had rattled her, however despite his fears, he did not believe he had made the wrong choice. Hadn't Alex suggested he tell her his plans from the start?

With his other hand he tilted her chin so he could gaze into her eyes. To his surprise he did not see the recognition he had expected, only hesitancy and perhaps some confusion. He sighed in relief as perhaps he would be able to execute his plan after all. Time would tell, of course.

"Anna, you are understandably confused by the change in plans. If you would allow me to begin, all will become clear. But you must be patient, my love."

Anna's eyes widened, but she did not speak. *Of course, now would be the time that she remembered the rules!*

"For this event you will be permitted to speak. In fact, I encourage it. Do you understand?"

She shook her head. "No, no— I do not. Did I do something wrong? Am I being sent away from Maitland House?"

He cursed. "Not at all, my dear. You have learned well over the last few days, and it is your progress that has initiated this change in plans for this day."

"I will be able to complete my *Awakening*?"

"But of course. That has never been in question. You have paid Maitland House handsomely to achieve what your heart desires." *As long as it is with me!*

A small hint of a smile crossed her lips, and she gently squeezed the fingers holding hers. "My Lord, you have no idea how relieved I am to hear that. However, I am still confused. What is the purpose of this event?" She turned her head from side to side indicating the crowd. "Who are these people?"

"You have asked questions about my life and the way I live."

"I mean you no disrespect Master J."

"This afternoon you may refer to me as Sir. This is a social occasion."

"As you wish, Sir. I still have questions."

"Exactly. Which is why I have brought my friends here. You do not have to take me at my word, you are able to observe and ask questions in a safe place."

"'Observe'?"

"Yes. These people present all have relationships such as what I have been exploring with you this week. You have the opportunity to have all your questions answered. You may ask anything you desire to know."

He saw the small dimple form on the left side of her mouth, and he was taken back to a time when she would share a joke and an impish grin with him while they rode together across his parents' land, hiding from her parents.

"Within reason of course. As you wish for your own privacy to be protected, so do my friends."

"My apologies, but I will ensure I am considerate."

"No offense taken lovely Anna. I was merely explaining the boundaries of the discussions. Having said that, if my friends wish to share information with you, then that is their own prerogative. We are a protective group, given the current state of the laws."

"I understand, and I promise I will respect your guests, Sir."

"I have never doubted that you would. Now come with me and I will make the introductions."

Although he schooled himself against reacting, he shivered as the soft silk of Anna's gown came in fluttered against his trousers. She did not appear to have noticed as he steered her towards the first group of guests. Her face was a study in concentration as they halted.

"Sir Alfred Penshurst and Lady Kathryn Penshurst, may I present Lady Anna Chamberlain."

One of his oldest friends, and his mentor nodded and smiled warmly. Although he had been introduced to the beauty of dominance and submission while on the Continent, it was this man who had truly opened his eyes to how it could be the basis of permanent and loving relationship. Since meeting him and his lovely wife he'd begun to make plans for a future with Anna. It had been a frustratingly long time when he could not contact her due to her controlling family, and at times he felt he would never find a way, but now they had a second chance and he intended to use all available resources to win her back.

"It is a pleasure to meet you, Lady Anna."

As he took her hand and kissed her fingers, Anna gasped and tried to retrieve her hand, but his old friend held firm.

"You must never refuse a compliment from an old man, young lady."

Her cheeks turned pink, and she smiled. "When I meet an old man, I will be sure to remember that sir."

Alfred, although not usually prone to public displays of emotion, laughed loudly. He patted Justin on the back as he regained his breath. "Well done my friend. She lives up to your description quite nicely."

He watched her intently for any reaction to his friend's comments, but all he could see was her smile.

"Do I get to say anything?"

Alfred turned to his wife. "Of course, my love. Say something lovely and soothing for this frightened lamb."

"I do not believe for a minute she is frightened," she said, taking Anna's hand from her husband. "Welcome to our friendship circle Lady Anna. I am certain that we will be seeing a lot of each other in the future. I have a very good feeling about that."

"You are too kind, both of you," said Anna. "But please, I am not accustomed to being referred to as Lady. You may call me Anna."

"Nonsense," said Lady Penshurst. "My understanding is that you have recently become an heiress, and independent financially. I also believe you cared for your ailing father for many years. Anyone who displays that much devotion to duty and sacrifice deserves to be given a title. Even one as mild as *Lady*. You deserve it."

"I only did what any daughter should do for her family, but I thank you for the generous words. I do not believe that I have done anything more that many others have before me," said Anna.

"My wife has very definite ideas about the place of women in society. Especially as we have an independent thinking Queen for a monarch."

"I do admire our monarch, however I do not agree with all of her politics, my dear. As you well know."

Sir Alfred winked at Anna. "I do love to stir her up. She is full of fire, even after all these years."

"You both appear to be well-versed in my history; however, I know naught of yours. How long have you been married?"

"We have been together for thirty-five years, my dear."

Anna gasped, her beautiful lips forming a circle of surprise. "That is quite an accomplishment".

Justin interrupted at that moment. This was not meant to be a conversation of mere pleasantries, but more an evening of discovery. "Anna, do you have any questions to ask Lord and Lady Penshurst?"

"I did not wish to be too forward, nor do I do wish to offend."

"Perfectly fine, my dear. Ask away. It is in fact the reason we are here," said Lady Penshurst. "If you prefer, the men can spend some time finding us some refreshments while you and I get to know each other. Would that be acceptable?" She looked at her husband, her eyebrow raised.

Alfred nodded discreetly, but Justin noted that Anna caught that slight movement of approval. Her shoulders seem to relax, and she smiled. "To be honest Lady Kathryn, I feel that would be better. I am at heart a very shy person." Anna turned her face to Justin and smiled. "That is of course if it is acceptable to Master J?"

He nodded. "Certainly Anna. However, I suggest you reserve the option for you to ask questions of others present before this evening is done."

Anna glanced around the room in surprise. "Are all these people like yourself?"

Justin smiled down at her. He was starting to relax as it

appeared she had not yet recognised him. He knew it was only a matter of time, however until that moment he could show her the beauty and joy of what could be. "But of course. They are here at the invitation of Alexandr and myself, to assist you on your journey to *Awakening*."

She clutched at his hand, stroking her soft fingers across his palm. Her eyes shone. "I thank you Master J. I am grateful for the opportunity to complete my time here."

His skin tingled where her hand had been, and he missed the touch. "There was never any question that you would complete your quest, my lady." He bowed to her and turned to Alfred.

"Off we go, Alfie—the ladies have much to discuss."

"Of course, dear boy. Lead on."

As he led his old friend to the table laden with delicacies, he prayed she would forgive the subterfuge. It was his only hope for the life he dreamed of.

* * *

Anna took a deep breath as she settled herself in the chair on the open veranda outside the parlour where she had left the guests. Lady Kathryn sat next to her in silence while she collected her thoughts. The days she had been here at Maitland House had been surprising and, in a way, very exhilarating, and this in part was due to the feeling of apprehension of the act that was to be the final moment of her stay. She was to end this week no longer a virgin and that thought alone was terrifying, but to not know the person with whom she was to be initiated was another thing entirely. She had not known how much this was affecting her until the moment she had entered the room and learned the identity of the man who had shown her so much about herself. It had been a shock to realise the man who had taken such care of her the past few days was Justin, her childhood love. Although she was unsure of how this came to be, she should not be surprised how safe he made her feel. The one who, when she closed her eyes imagined doing these wicked things to her body, and now she knew he was indeed the one who was doing them.

Lady Kathryn reached over and touched Anna's arm softly. "You know who he is, my dear."

"Yes, I do."

Lady Katherine's smile lit up her face. "I knew it. I knew from how you looked at him. How long have you known?"

"In my heart, I feel that since the first touch my whole being recognised him, but my brain did not want to acknowledge, for fear that I was mistaken. It was only when I returned to the parlour just now that I knew the truth."

"You are to be congratulated my dear Anna. You did not betray yourself in the slightest."

"And yet you yourself have guessed, my lady."

"Ah, but I am known for my intuition, Anna. I notice things."

"If you noticed, then perhaps others have as well. Do you think Justin is aware?"

The sound of her companion's laughter was enough to warm her heart. Although similar in age to her mother, should she still be alive, she appeared as young at heart as Gemma, one of the maids at Maitland House.

"Justin is a man. They do not notice subtlety. He is worried you will not understand."

"And yet he was without his mask this evening? Surely, he wanted me to discover his identity?"

"Yes, it appears he did."

"But why would he choose to wait until now to tell me? Why did he not reveal himself at the start of my time here?"

"You will need to ask that question of Justin my dear. It is the discussion you both need to have in private. It is not for me to speak of his thoughts."

"He has spoken of me then?"

"He has discussed your wishes for this week, and that he had known you as a child. The rest of what he desires is only conjecture on our part."

"'Conjecture'?"

"Yes, I believe I am a good judge of character and people's motives. I can certainly see what Justin is planning. And for all of the right reasons."

"And what would the right reasons be?"

"Ah...you will need to speak to Justin. I urge you to listen with your heart."

"I am very confused, Lady Kathryn."

Lady Kathryn moved closer to Anna and put her arms around her. "My dear, it most certainly has been a shock. Whatever you decide will take great courage. But remember, you have shown incredible strength in putting your desires first in your life and requesting an *Awakening* from Alexandr. It is this inner knowledge that will guide you to know what is best."

"But I do not know of what I need to decide. I only know that what I have found here at these past days is something I do not want to leave behind."

"Then don't."

"How can I know what it is that I should choose until I know what it is Justin wants?"

"Ah, but that is the beauty, my dear. You have all the power. Whatever you decide will be a gift to Justin."

"But what if he doesn't wish to continue after this week?"

Lady Kathryn chuckled. "You must trust me when I say this, my dear. Justin has waited his whole life for you. He will not let you go easily. But it *must* be your decision. It should be what you want, and not because you believe it is expected of you, or that Justin coerces you into it."

Anna shivered, although the night chill had yet to descend. She crossed her arms around her middle and moved forward on her seat. "I know that I will never again fulfil anyone else's desires except my own. My parents took away my choices when I was growing up. Now that I have the means to support myself, it will be *me* who will decide."

"Well said my dear."

"But does the life Justin desires with me mean subservience? I'm not sure I could live with that. Not after all I've experienced with my family."

"Oh Anna. It certainly does *not* mean subservience."

"If not subservience, then *what*?"

"Let me explain. Men such as my Alfred, and your Justin—they are strong men, but their greatest desire is to care deeply for the woman they love. Women such as myself, and from what I have seen—you also, we need to feel free from all the worries and stresses in our lives, and one way for us to experience that is give over control to another. In doing so we are giving the greatest gift of all in the name of love. We are giving our complete trust."

"When you explain it like that it sounds wonderful, but how do you live every day in the control of another? Do you not want to make decisions for yourself? Be free to do as you wish?"

"But I am free to do whatever I wish. Alfred knows that I am an independent woman with intelligence and opinions. He encourages me to express them. I am able to come and go as I please, except forwhen we are in the bedroom. But that is always dependent on my choice. I'm the one who chooses to allow him to care for me."

"So, you are the one with the power?"

"Exactly! Alfred cannot care for me without my permission. And I can remove that permission at any time."

"And what of your servants? Friends?"

"Our servants are discreet. And the friends who are aware of our proclivities are also members of Maitland House. Our other acquaintances may be curious, but do not ask questions, as it should be."

"Thank you for your candour, Lady Kathryn. Do you mind if I ask a few more questions of a personal nature?"

"Why of course. This is why I am here."

"Do you have children? Are they aware of how their parents live?"

"Yes, we have a son and a daughter. Both know of the philosophy of our life, but we ensured to protect them, hence we keep our activities to our bedroom."

"And this choice of life makes you happy?"

Lady Kathryn smiled serenely. "Blissfully. And I'm

confident that should you wish to pursue a similar relation-ship with Justin, you will also be thus. But the question is are you able to forgive Justin for deceiving you?"

"I will admit, I am very confused by all of this. I had a plan for my life now that I'm free of the bonds of my parents. I thought my childhood dreams of a life with Justin were gone. Now all of that is in disarray. I can't make any decisions at the present time."

"Am I correct then, in discerning that you may be think-ing of a life with Justin given the questions you have asked of me?"

"I would be wrong to say that I have not thought of continuing the experiences I've had these last few days. I do not know if it is Justin who is the way forward for me, but before this week I would not have questioned this. Too much has happened, in particular over the last hour. All my beliefs of what I thought my life is—has now been thrown into dis-array. I will need time to think."

Lady Kathryn took Anna's hands into hers. "I understand completely my dear. The evening has brought with it many surprises. But please remember at the heart of all of this, Justin loves you. I ask that you give him the opportunity to tell you his story before you judge him too harshly."

"I promise that I will listen. I wish to know his motives, but I cannot promise that I will be able to forgive him"

"Listening is a good start," said Lady Kathryn as she stood. "Shall we return to the men and see what delicacies they have collected for us? I do not know about you, but I find myself very hungry."

Anna smiled, albeit nervously. If she could delay returning

to Justin she would, but she knew it was putting off the inevitable, so she took a deep breath, straightened her shoulders, and together they walked back into the parlour.

* * *

Justin clenched his hand against his thigh while listening to Alfred regale him of tales of the country house and the recent foxhunt. It was difficult trying to keep his mind on the conversation when all he wanted was to know what Anna was asking of Lady Kathryn. Did she want another of Alexandr's staff to complete her *Awakening*? Would she be open to continuing a relationship with him after her week at Maitland House was over? Would she stay or had he ruined his chances and scared her away? Would she ever forgive him?

"Oh, here they are my boy. Just in time," said Alfred.

Justin felt his heart skip a beat as Lady Kathryn and Anna returned. He stood and made a space for Anna to sit, while Alfred did the same for Lady Kathryn. "We have taken the liberty of preparing a feast for you both. We hope your conversation was fruitful."

Justin saw Lady Kathryn wink at Anna. "I believe so."

Anna's face flushed a pretty shade of pink.

"Anna, did you learn what you sought?" he asked.

She raised her face towards him, but did not meet his eyes. "I have gained some information, but there is more I do not know. Unfortunately, I believe each answer has brought new questions."

"That is to be expected. This is a journey best experienced over time," he said. What was he saying? He sounded like an ass. Worse still, a stuck-up ass.

"What Justin means is that life involves new experiences

along the way. It is not possible to know what each day will bring. Is that correct, James?" said Lady Kathryn.

"Thank you, Lady Kathryn. You have a more poetic turn of phrase than I."

Damn. Kathryn referred to him by his own name. Had Anna recognised him after all? Why had she not said anything?

"You are welcome, Justin," she said, as she picked up a strawberry from the platter in front of her. "Anna, I trust you have gained a greater insight?"

Anna lifted her head. "Oh yes, Lady Kathryn. You have been most helpful. I have much to think about."

Justin ate in silence, biding his time until he could speak to Anna in private. He wanted her to get the most benefit from this evening so once his plate was empty, he returned it to the table and placed his hand on Anna's shoulder. She shivered at his touch, and he hoped that was a good sign of where her feelings lay. "My dear, there are many others here tonight who would be more than happy to answer any further questions you may have. The night is not yet finished, and it would be a pity to waste the opportunity in front of you."

"Do not put undue pressure on the girl Justin," said Alfred.

"That is not my intention..."

"It is not necessary for you to defend me, Lord Alfred, but I thank you for your care," said Anna. She turned towards Justin, avoiding his eyes by staring at her clenched hands on her lap. "I have learned many unexpected truths this evening Justin," she said. "Although I do sincerely appreciate your offer to introduce me to the other guests, my mind is so full of information that my head is spinning."

"Of course, my dear," said Lady Kathryn. "You have much to consider." She stood and held her hand out to Anna. "Come. I will escort you to your room."

Anna clasped her hand and rose to join her. "I would be very grateful for your company my lady."

Justin swore as they left the room. That did not go well at all, and he feared his plans were now completely awry.

A clink of glass drew him back to the company beside him. Sir Alfred was refreshing his brandy and snickering at him.

"Don't worry my boy. She will come around."

"I have no idea what she is thinking, but the Anna I remember would find it difficult to forgive any subterfuge. I have deceived her from the start."

"Nonsense Justin. You forget I have seen the way she looks at you when you are not watching. She needs time, but all will be well. I am sure of it."

"I wish I had your confidence, old friend. I should have approached her directly as soon as I knew of her wish to attend here."

"But that would have deprived her of the experience she craved. Do you think she would have been open to this life if you had suggested it without her time here?"

"Indeed, that is what I was trying to achieve. In no way did I want to interfere with her wishes. But to do that I lied to her. Perhaps I should have waited until this week was over before making my overtures."

"Ha! Could you have lived with her experiencing the entire *Awakening* without you? Have another be the first to initiate her?"

"No. That's the problem. I thought I could, but once I saw how she responded, it had to be me."

"There. You have your answer."

"But what if she cannot forgive me?"

"She will. She has not forgotten you, even after all these years."

"And I have never thought of anyone else."

"Then all will be well. Have faith in your love."

Justin sighed. "I will definitely try."

"And don't rush her. She'll come to you when she is ready."

"I will endeavour to take your advice, but it will be difficult."

"I suggest you leave and return tomorrow afternoon. It will allow her time to think it through, and to ask any questions she may still have. I am certain Alexandr will be more than willing to look out for her on your behalf."

Justin groaned. "That is what I fear. He is already attracted to her."

Lord Alfred laughed. "Any man would appreciate such a beauty. However, you should observe in which direction our host's eyes wander when a certain female enters the room."

"Surely he is not developing a *tendre* for a client?"

"Oh no, he is much too careful of that kind of behaviour, my young friend."

Justin turned in the direction of Lord Alfred's gaze and smiled.

"Ah, I see."

"I have said too much. I am sure he fights the inevitable, but like you, my young friend, both of you are only hurting yourselves if you do not follow your destiny."

"Yes, but what if my destiny is at odds with my love's and our paths do not join?"

"Then this is not your true destiny, and I do not believe that is the case. Have faith. It will all work out as it is meant to be."

"I trust that you are correct, my learned friend. Because for half of my lifetime I have waited for this. I cannot allow myself to think of an alternative."

"Go now and give your young beauty the space she needs," said Lord Alfred. "I will deal with Alexandr and ensure she is well protected until your return."

Justin nodded. "Indeed, I shall follow your advice, but know this is very difficult when my first impulse is to run after her and explain all."

"Of course it is, but you both need the time apart to think through all that has happened. Not just these past few days, but over the years you have been apart. When you meet again you will know what to say."

"I pray you are correct my friend."

"I am always right Justin. My Lady Kathryn will vouch for that!"

6

Chapter Six

Maitland House

My dearest Justin

Words cannot convey the enormity of my feelings at this present moment. To find that you are here in London, and not married off and living on the continent as I was led to believe has been a shock. I assumed this to be the case, as my parents told me it was so. I have come to understand that many of things they told me over the years were surely untruths. Lies designed for them to maintain their control over me. I know you foresaw this happening when we were young, and we were just finding out what love was, but my parents were so very threatened by your presence in my life. Looking back, I can see more clearly how they intervened, lied, and withheld information. I originally thought it was because they wanted me to wed a Lord or a Duke, and not a second son such as yourself, but I no longer believe that. The truth is they did not want marriage for me to anyone. It suited them to have me under their direct control, and now I am out from that constrained, suffocating and subservient existence, I am filled with a sense of freedom. I can finally breathe. Something I did not realise I struggled with until the cause was no longer there.

However, I find myself filled with pity for my parents. What a sad life they made for themselves where they needed to control their child to such an extent to find their own happiness. So, despite the loss of the life I would have wanted for myself, I do forgive them. That is not to say I do not have many regrets for what could have been, but as you have most likely surmised, in coming here to Maitland House, I am determined to put measures in place to rectify some of those missed experiences I have not undertaken. I fully understand I have reached an age where most women have been married with several children already born, so it comes to mind that some of my previous dreams will require some changes.

Which leads me to the reason I am writing to you. Being here at Maitland House this week has been an illuminating experience for me. One I never thought to have. I have discovered many things about myself and my body that in my wildest dreams I would never have known. I had thought to be cognisant of many tales of the erotic, spending many hours of my time reading forbidden books I had purloined from the servants, as I was locked in my bedchamber each evening at my parents' home. However, reading and looking upon artistic impressions did not prepare me for the emotions or the sensations I have experienced these past few days. For that I thank you.

You could have stopped me, or worse, let me know your identity on that first day, and as you no doubt surmised, I would have fled in fright at being found in this position. You saved me from that, and I understand why you did it.

What I do not understand is what I wish to do with this newfound knowledge. And it is for this reason that I have decided to leave Maitland House immediately. I will not be completing my Awakening. I have sent a note to Master Alexandr advising him of my wishes.

Please do not follow me. I will find you once I have made my decision.

You remain my oldest and dearest friend, and I am overjoyed to have found you again, however I have much to think about, and I know not where my thoughts and feelings will finish. I pray I will come to a decision which will give us both peace.

Love always,
Anna

* * *

Justin sat back down in the soft leather Grandfather chair he'd inherited from his father. He stared at the crumpled the letter in his hand. He lifted his arm, aiming for the fire but at the last minute he stopped himself from destroying the one thing he had left that Anna had touched. He smoothed the letter against his thigh in an attempt to remove the creases. He read the words again, although he knew what they said. He'd read it countless times in the month since he'd first received it—a month he'd spent soul-searching and damning himself for his impatience. However, he refused to give up hope. Not after all these years when fate had given him the opportunity to be with the one woman he could never forget.

He closed his eyes and remembered his Anna as she shivered with pleasure at his touch. She was reacting honestly and that gave him something to hold on to. Her letter indicated she understood why he had deceived her but given all the untruths her parents had told her over the years, he was concerned that over time she would not be able to forgive him. Most of her life she had been lied to, and now the person she should have been able to trust the most had done the same. He certainly did not forgive himself for his deeds.

Oh, how he had marvelled when she appeared to embrace his proclivities. She hadn't shied away, although at times she had appeared to hesitate. No, she was the strong and brave woman he always knew she would grow up to be. And beautiful. Yes, so beautiful.

The sound of the door to his library opening drew him from his reverie.

Alexandr Sokoloff burst into the room "Justin, my friend." he said. "Where in blazes have you been hiding yourself?"

"I see you still feel the need to barge into rooms, Alex. One would have thought you had grown out of that habit after Eton."

"Ha! How else was I to get in to see you. You've been ignoring my overtures for weeks."

"My apologies, Alex. I have not been in the mood for company of late. I instructed my staff to let no one in."

"I'm slightly offended by that, but you can make it up to me by pouring me a glass of your very fine port."

Justin couldn't help but smile. Alexandr was, as always, a very good friend and perhaps he could do with the company of a friend this evening. He reached for the crystal carafe on his desk and poured two glasses. He took a glass to his friend and kept one for himself, swallowing a large portion in one fell swoop.

Alexandr narrowed his eyes and stared at him. "I don't remember you to be of the mind to wallow Justin. It does not sit well on you. I believe you are in dire need of a barber and a valet."

Justin ran his fingers through his unruly hair and sighed, turning towards the window. "I find myself questioning all my actions when it comes to Anna. I have waited for word from her for one month but have heard nothing. I am convinced she has decided to stay out of my life forever and continue her on her ways to experience the life she has missed. Allow me this time to wallow my friend. I am mourning the loss of my love."

"Balderdash! You're not usually the one to give up so easily by friend. Look at how you planned for your lady love's visit to my establishment. It was precise and reeked of determination to win. Why has that changed now? Why don't you go after what you want?"

Justin turned back to face his friend. "Because she asked me not to."

"Tsk. That's not a reason to give up."

"But also, because she spent her whole life doing what others told her to. I owe her the opportunity to make her own decisions. Follow her own paths."

"That is surely a noble reason to leave her be, but what if her lack of experience in life means she does not really know what she wants? What if she needs someone, she can trust to help her to see the truth?"

"It is not quite as simple as that, Alex."

"It surely is, Justin. I believe if you want her in your life, you will find a way to convince her. You have naught to lose. At this present time, you are alone and without her. If she rebuffs you, nothing changes. But imagine if you can show her how much she means to you? You have spent your whole life waiting for her." He crossed the room and placed his hand on Justin's shoulder. "Do not give up on your dreams, my friend. You will have many regrets if you do."

"I already do."

Alexandr drained his glass and placed it on the tray on Justin's desk. "Just promise me that you will think on all that I have said."

"Believe me, I have already thought of each one of the possibilities you have brought to me."

Alexandr held his hand up. "I have said my piece now. The rest is up to you."

"I have already made my choice."

Alexandr smiled at him. "Ah, but have you? Really?" He turned to leave but paused at the door. "Dobre nochi, moy drook" *Good night my friend.*

Justin removed the crumpled note from his pocket and opened it once more. As he read it again, he thought of all that Alex had said. How he did not have much to lose if he went in search of his love. But his insecurities set in. What if she couldn't forgive him for keeping his identity a secret? What if his actions had destroyed any feeling, she may have kept in her heart for him? But then he thought about never knowing the answers to these questions and he knew what he had to do.

Now he had a course of action he wanted to follow; he needed a meticulous plan. Strategy had always been one of his strengths, and he needed to use it now. If he didn't do this right, it could be the end of his journey to happiness forever.

* * *

7

Chapter Seven

The sun shone brightly through the trees as Anna walked the well-worn path in the woods beyond her home. She loved her Tudor cottage with its thatched roof, and never failed to smile when she gazed upon its tranquil setting. Nettie, her maid, and Joseph, her wonderful gardener were the only links to her previous life. She could not bear to leave them behind as they were the sole friends she'd had while she cared for her parents. And since she had brought them here, they revealed to her that they had been secretly married for years. Her parents had frowned on such liaisons, so they had been frightened to make that knowledge public, however now her parents had died, and they had moved to Gloucestershire with her, they were free to live the life they deserved. This made her happy.

Anna had sold the family estate and bought this small property after leaving Maitland House, realising she needed a complete break from her past. Since arriving she had settled into the tranquil environment with enthusiasm and happiness. Joseph, it appeared, was a genius when it came to roses and had created a stunning walled rose garden, with tumbling masses of fragrant pink, yellow and white roses that made her heart sing.

But despite the peace she had found in this place, she remained unsettled. Since leaving her experience at Maitland House behind, she felt a yearning she never thought she would have. It was not that she wished to partake in all the wanton activities offered there. Of course, she had been shocked at her reactions and desires—there had never before been such pleasure in her life. It could become addictive. Therefore she must take care before she took part again. Before Justin had confessed his duplicitous role, she hadn't been sure what she'd wanted, but once he came back into her life, even though she initially didn't know it was him—somehow her heart knew. It had felt right. But after his revelations, she had panicked and left, and was not sure if she could trust either Justin, or her own feelings. It had been almost three months now, and she was yet to know her own mind. And it disconcerted and confused her.

She had spent her whole life being controlled by her parents, and now she was free to choose her own way, she had discovered she felt a deep desire to be controlled, at least when it came to the erotic. How could this be? What was wrong with her? She knew many people felt the same desires as her, and despite the secrecy and protection of those who enjoyed these so-called *"proclivities"*, these feelings were not all that uncommon. Her secret books had taught her that, so she should not have been surprised. However, she didn't know if this was something she could live with for the rest of her life? Not now when it was just beginning.

As she made her way along the path she came to her favourite place. It was a few minutes' walk past the rose garden and had an exquisite view of the valley below. The small wrought iron table and chairs sat under the canopy of a large London plane tree, which at this time of the year gave a welcome shade from the summer heat. She retrieved her notebook from the pocket of her apron and headed towards one of the chairs then stopped. It seemed someone had been there before her.

The table was covered by a linen cloth and decorated with a single yellow rose. Standing against the small vase was a letter addressed to Anna and a small package lay beside it.

Anna glanced around her, and examined in front and behind the tree, searching for signs of anyone who could have set the table.

"Is anyone there?"

The one sound she heard was the melodic song of a willow warbler as it flitted from branch to branch above her head.

A gust of wind swirled around her skirt and kissed her legs under her petticoat, making her shiver and the wind lifted the letter off the table and it landed on the leafy carpet below. She picked it up, turning it over a few times in search of a clue to who may have written it. Seeing none, she sat and opened it.

The note was a single sheet of paper, and as she drew closer, she caught a wisp of spice when she opened it.

* * *

My darling Anna,

*I have your likeness in my mind and my heart every night,
and I long, with impatience for you to make your decision.
This has become more difficult as the time passes. I have
been sitting alone most evenings and waiting on your word,
although it is not my intention to press you. However, I
wanted to remind you that not once in all these years have
I ever forgotten you. I have left a token to show you how
much this is true.*

    Until I hear from you,

    Yours,

    Justin

* * *

Anna stared at the note for a few minutes and closed
her eyes. Justin. The man she'd dreamed of for so long. The
man with who she now had the opportunity she had always
wanted, but now the time had come, she was more confused
than ever. Perhaps she should open the box and see what it
was he had given her.

The box was small and tied with a white ribbon. She
removed the wrapping and opened it to find a silver locket
on a chain. The design was intricate with swirls and flowers
engraved on the front, while the back was embossed with just
one word—*Anna*. She pressed the small catch and the locket
sprung open to reveal a miniature painting. She recognised
it at once. It was a picture of her childhood pony, Bastian.

Justin had promised he would commission a piece for her when he received his small allowance from his father, but that was before he went away. She assumed now that her parents had made sure she would not see him again. But for all these years, she had believed he had put family duty ahead of their budding love. Now she knew better, although it still did not help her to decide. Many years had gone by since those young hearts had wished for more.

She gazed at the likeness of her beloved pony and smiled, remembering the stolen moments riding across the fields on her parents' estate. Moments that had given her so much joy.

Thank you, Justin, for reminding me of that wonderful time.

She closed the locket and placed the chain around her neck. The silver was warm against her skin and her heart lifted ever so slightly.

On her walk back to her cottage, she picked it up and held it in her hand several times, amazed at how much it had lifted her mood. Justin had known the exact thing to gift her. But one thoughtful gift did not make her decision any easier. There were many other aspects to think about, and if he was to be believed, after a lifetime of waiting, he could wait a little bit longer.

The next few days included the delivery of several small gifts. A box of her favourite fondants, a beautiful doll clothed in a dress exactly like the one she'd worn that last night at Maitland House, a pair of sapphire drop earrings to match that dress, and her absolute favourite—a corgi puppy. She named him Sebastian after her long-gone pony, and he had fast become her constant companion, running beside her with his tiny little legs as she walked each morning, and sleeping in a small bed of woollen blankets in her bedchamber at night.

On the morning of the seventh day since the first gift had arrived, a carriage drew up in front of the cottage and out stepped Justin. She wasn't surprised given the gifts, but now that she saw him standing in her garden with the sun shining on his unruly hair and as handsome and as confident as she remembered him, he took her breath away.

She took a step towards him, and his face lit up in a smile. "Justin."

He bowed his head and removed his hat. "Anna."

"You did not wait for me to write to you with my decision."

His eyes sparkled as he closed the gap between them and enfolded her in his arms. "I could not. For now that I have found you, I am unable to stay away, my love."

Before she could answer, he kissed her. Although it lasted a mere few seconds, her heart skipped a beat and the skin of her lips tingled. Oh, this man knew how to befuddle her brain. She pushed out of his arms and stepped back.

"Justin! I have yet to decide, so please do not muddy the waters for me."

Justin laughed. "I would not dream of it. However, if my presence will help you resolve in my favour than I will never apologise for that."

"You are incorrigible! I asked you to give me time."

"In my defence, I have a number of points I wanted to share with you before you made your final decision."

"And apparently you are not opposed to bribery either, judging by the array of gifts you have sent me these past few days."

"You did not like them?"

"No, the opposite is true. I love them. Especially Sebastian. But that is not the point. It blurs the argument."

"You named him after Bastian? May I see him?"

At the sound of his name, the golden ball of fluff who was Sebastian came bounding out from behind Anna's skirt.

Justin crouched and held out his hand as the puppy launched itself at him, jumped into his arms and began licking his face.

"I see you remember me, you little scamp," said Justin, cradling the small bundle in his arms.

Anna's heart melted as she watched the interaction between this grown man she had known as a boy, and the puppy he had given her. Seeing Justin in the flesh acting so playful reminded her of the life she had always dreamed of but had never believed was for her. Perhaps it *was* possible now, but this was the side of Justin she remembered. His other side she was only now discovering. It was his other side she wasn't sure about. Not able to grasp if she could live with the complexities and yes, the constraints. Constraints she did not wish to have. Not now she had her own money, home, and ability to make decisions about her own life.

"Why so serious, my little one?"

Anna shook her head slightly. "I am not being serious Justin. I am contemplating life, and all its treasures."

Justin laughed. "Of course," he said as he continued petting the doting puppy. "There is much to be thankful for."

"Yes, there is. I am finding more joy in each day, now that I am in the home of my choosing." She laughed and threw her arms wide. "This is my own piece of the world and I still pinch myself every day that this has come to pass."

"I am so happy for you Anna, my little rebel. I know the toll it must have taken, being subservient to your parents. I do have one question though, if you do not mind my asking."

"Of course, Justin. You can ask me anything."

"I mean no disrespect here, but once I discovered you again, and found out what your life became after I left, I cannot help but wonder why it was that you stayed with them."

Anna drew her arms across her chest and raised her chin. "What would you have had me do, Justin? I was an unmarried girl with no means of support. I had no desire to end up in the poor house or on the streets. It is different for a man. You can join the military. Women do not have that option."

"But you could have asked one of your friends or relatives for assistance?"

"My parents ensured I did not have any friends. My parents had no family I was aware of. Our servants became my companions instead, and I stayed because I had no alternative. I made the best of the situation."

Justin's raised an eyebrow. "I have the utmost admiration for you Anna. You have lived a life filled with many difficulties, yet here you are living an independent life and still caring for all those around you. I am in awe of your resilience."

Anna felt a warm tingling that swept up the back of her neck and across her face. Damn her habit of blushing in his presence, however, his words did please her.

"In fact," continued Justin. "It is the maintenance of your new independence and the ability to make your own decisions I wanted to discuss with you."

Anna turned her head, unable to meet Justin's gaze. She feared this moment as it could mean she would be forced to choose to either abandon her dreams or compromise her morals. Every way she considered it, she could not see a way this would end well for either of them. She needed more time to explore her feelings and all she had experienced at Maitland House.

"I'm not sure I am ready to hear your thoughts on this, Justin."

Justin gently placed Sebastian back down on the ground. The lively puppy quickly trotted towards the cottage and towards a water bowl where he could be heard enthusiastically lapping at the water.

"Do not fear, Anna. My only wish is to allay your concerns and reassure you they are entirely unfounded."

"How would you know of my concerns, since I have yet to voice them?" she said. "In fact, I am not so sure that I have thought them through myself."

"Perhaps I can be of assistance in that regard."

"In what way?"

"I can explain what I have in mind for an ongoing relationship, and you will then have the opportunity to ask questions. You left Maitland House before I had a chance to make my thoughts clear on this."

"It is all very strange, Justin."

Justin took her hand in his, the warmth of his skin almost a comfort when he lifted it to his mouth and kissed her palm. "I know my life is a mystery to you, my love. And as a young single woman who has lived such a sheltered life, the recent events must have come as a shock, however you must have had an inkling of what might be, to have arranged your sojourn in the first place."

Anna blushed. "My wish was to relieve myself of my virginity. It was my belief that love, and marriage were things I would never experience. This was an opportunity for me to have a glimpse of what others had."

Justin's eyes sparkled. "I think you were expecting more than that, otherwise you would have run in fright at that first meeting with Alexandr."

She lowered her eyes again. "It is true I suspected there was more. I had read forbidden novels and secretly viewed drawings of an erotic nature. However, what you and I did together, that is nothing like I would have ever thought possible."

"But you liked it."

Anna blushed at the memories, and the heat in her cheeks increased. "I admit it was pleasurable, but I am still uncertain if I could continue along the same path. I am now only finding my confidence. Why would I want to become supplicant to another?"

"I do not wish for a slave, Anna. I want a partner in life. Your blossoming confidence is what has convinced me that we are perfect for each other."

"But what of your *proclivities*?"

"Ah." A light appeared in Justin's eyes as he smiled at her. "You are under the mistaken impression that I would have you naked and restrained at all times."

"Well, yes. That did cross my mind. And I know for a certainty—*that* is not something I could live with. I had enough of control and restrictions while my parents were alive. At

Maitland House, it was a fantasy where I was in control. It was temporary. But in truth, I want to live my life in the real world."

"And I would not want it any other way."

Her eyes widened. "Then exactly what is it that you are proposing, Justin?"

Justin gestured to the garden chairs on the terrace. "Please, take a seat. I do not wish you to be uncomfortable while we discuss what I have in mind."

Anna chose the garden bench, which was closest to the pathway to the house, lest she needed to make a swift egress. She sat, adjusting her skirts and positioned herself on the edge of the seat. "Fine. I am seated."

Justin's mouth curled up with the hint of a smile as his eyes never left hers. He settled himself on the wicker chair after moving it to close the distance between them. His closeness was unsettling, but she could not say she was unhappy with the flutter circling her heart.

Justin reached out and with a feather light touch, brushed a finger over her cheek. She leaned into his palm as it replaced his finger. Her skin tingled and a warmth spread throughout her body. And this from a brief touch? *How on Earth will I be able to resist him?*

"Firstly," he said. "I can tell you that yes, my proclivities will remain. However, I find myself very fond of seeing you blossom and take control of your own destiny. Your parents were cruel, but you have risen above this. I do not wish in any way to make you feel any less than yourself. You deserve to be in control of your destiny.

"But how?"

Justin placed a finger over her lips. "Wait, and hear the rest of it," he said. "I truly believe you share many of the same desires as I. Your time at Maitland House must have shown you that, but I do understand why you have been frightened by this. I believe I have the solution that will be satisfactory for both of us. What I am proposing will allow you to have control, but also to be enable us to have both our fantasies fulfilled."

Anna turned her head to the side and sucked in a breath. What he said sounded wonderful, but she could not envisage how it would work. Much as she would adore it to, she did not hold much confidence that it was workable, or even possible. "That sounds all well and good Justin, but how is that even conceivable?"

"It is really quite simple my love. I understand you questioned Lady Kathryn about her life with Lord Alfred. What I am proposing is a similar arrangement. That our activities are for our eyes alone and occur in the privacy of our bedroom. And only with your agreement. I find I am ambivalent to anyone catching even a glimpse of your body. Those few days at Maitland House have taught me that I need you all to myself. Why do you think I insisted you were clothed for that last session?"

"To be honest Justin, I feared you had tired of me and did not want me to continue."

"Not at all, my love. Just the opposite. I did not want to share you with any other members of the Maitland House community, and more importantly, I did not want to put undue pressure on you through removing your choices."

"You did that for me?"

Justin nodded. "Yes, my love. Unfortunately, you left Maitland House before I had a chance to explain. So before you take the time to decide, I must explain what life I wish for the both of us. I have had almost a lifetime to imagine it, although for many years I believed you were lost to me. It is a miracle that you reappeared in my life, and I cannot let this opportunity slip through my fingers. Not after the way I was removed from you and our love in the past. Something I have always regretted. I should have fought harder for you, but I was young, inexperienced, and I believed the lies your parents told me. I should have realised their deception sooner, but instead I chose to run away to a life on another continent and as far away from you as I could."

"But what lie could my parents have told me that would lead you to those actions?"

"I was told you had married."

"What? Why would you believe them?"

"They showed me the announcement in the *Times*."

"That is impossible. I was never married."

"It was obviously a forgery. I know that now, but as a young man in love I was devastated to see what I felt was definitive proof in front of my eyes."

"Why did you not seek me out?"

"I tried but was told you and your new husband were traveling in Italy on your honeymoon. I believed it too late, and feared there was nothing I could do."

"My parents told you that many lies?"

"They did. And I am so angry with myself that I took their word as truth."

Anna reached for him, laying her hand gently on his forearm. "You were not to know, Justin."

"I should have questioned them. It was not the first time I had been visited by them to discourage my growing affection for you."

Anna's eyes filled with tears. "I knew my parents had aspirations for a good marriage, but I wasn't aware of their subterfuge."

"That was my first thought as well. But given what eventuated, I now believe they had no such plan. They wanted to keep you for themselves. They had no intention of allowing you to marry. They used you as their own personal slave."

Anna turned away, wiping the tears from her cheeks with her shaking hands. "You are correct. I came to the same conclusion myself. I was a prisoner in my home. My parents were my jailers."

"I'm so sorry Anna."

"Do not be, Justin. I am still reasonably young, free of them now. A woman of comfortable means and for the first time in my life, I can do as I please, and have no care for what others think."

"Which is why you decided to attend Maitland House?"

Anna looked down, the tell-tale sign of her embarrassment apparent in the pinking of her cheeks. "This is true."

"I cannot say I am sorry that you decided to follow that path, because it is what led you back to me, but I am curious as to why you would choose to put yourself in that precarious position?"

"Do you mean my reputation?"

"Exactly. Why would you gift your virginity to a stranger instead of a husband?"

Anna laughed. "I certainly have no expectation of marriage, Justin. I have only recently become free of the constraints of my family. Why would I tether myself to another person who would make decisions on my behalf when I have only discovered the joy of doing this for myself? No, that is not happening. However, I still had the desire to experience what I would miss. Hence this is why I purchased the *Awakening*."

"An experience that my presence interrupted."

"Yes," she whispered.

"I am so sorry you did not finish your *Awakening*, Anna, however my ego is pleased that that no other man has tasted what I desire."

"And what if I have decided to achieve my goal through other sources? What then, Justin?"

"I hope that will not be necessary my love. My dearest wish is you will listen to what I am proposing and will join me on the journey together."

"And still, you have yet to make clear just what it is you desire."

"I believe it was you who said you were not yet ready to decide."

"That may be true, however it is difficult to decide when one does not know what the choices are. I am not opposed to hearing what you have to say, however I cannot promise that you will be happy with my opinion."

"Are you sure you are ready to hear it, my love?"

Anna faced him front on; her face a picture of defiance. "I am as prepared as I will ever be, Justin. I can't move forward into my new life without knowledge of my choices. Although I *will* warn you. At this moment in my life, I am completely averse to having decisions taken for me".

Justin smiled, taking hold of her hands. She blushed as he rubbed his thumbs back and forth on the soft skin of her wrists. "Then you must listen closely my love, to what I am asking. Because the last thing I would ever intend would be to remove any decision from you. I am one of the only people left in London who knows what your parents were capable of and what they inflicted on you in their selfishness. You deserve to be adored, and free to experience all life has to offer without fear."

Anna attempted to pull her hands free, but Justin held firm. "Please wait and hear what I have to say."

She stopped struggling and rested her hands on her lap, "Please get to the point Justin."

"I'm so sorry my love. I speak in circles only because I am nervous of your decision."

"You do not strike me as a man who lacks confidence."

"Ah, but that is where you are wrong. My dreams are in your hands. You are the key, and my heart is the lock waiting to be opened."

"Ha! Since when did you speak such flowery words?"

He lifted her hand to his lips and kissed her knuckle. "You wound me. I have always felt deeply for you."

"But you moved out of my life a long time ago, Justin. Much has happened to both of us since we were young. We have changed."

"I have never once stopped thinking of you."

"Surely there were other women in your life?"

"I cannot deny it. I am no saint. However, none have meant as much to me as you, my little rebel."

Anna shivered as Justin stroked her hands with his thumbs.

"But I digress, my love. Do you recall your discussion with Lady Kathryn regarding her marriage?"

"The events of that evening are burned into my memory. I cannot forget the kindness she showed to me amidst all the confusion."

"And what do you remember of her and the relationship with Lord Alfred?"

"She struck me as the most independent of women and an equal with her husband."

"Exactly. Yet they still prefer the more exotic of intimate lifestyles in the privacy of their own company. Were you aware?"

"She did speak of it."

"And what were your thoughts? Is this something that you might consider?"

"Is that what you are suggesting for us?"

"Would that be a bad thing, my love?"

"But at Maitland House there were so many rules. I am not sure I could live that way. Not now that I have finally achieved some modicum of independence."

Justin shook his head. "Maitland House is a fantasy. I want a realistic life with a strong and independent woman. I want a life with you, my best friend."

"And you would not miss the rules? Being Master J?"

"Ah, I could still be your Master J. But only with your consent, if that is what you wish, and *only* in the bedchamber.

I have no desire to share my lovely bride with anyone else, other than myself. I want a partner in life, not a slave."

Anna stood abruptly, this time with no resistance from Justin. "I am very touched and honoured by your proposal, and you have given me much to think about, but I will need more time before I can answer you."

Justin rose to join her, the power and heat emanating from him a tangible thing as her emotions whirled inside her. She took a few steps back. "Please Justin, let me go so that I may breathe a little. I need a little solitude so I may think."

Justin bowed. "Of course. I am rushing you. But I feel as if I have waited my whole life for this moment and it makes me impatient." He smiled down at her as he tucked a stray curl behind her ear. She shivered and her head leaned towards his hand of its own volition. For her own sanity she quickly righted herself and took another few steps backwards, hoping the distance between them would be enough for her to refrain from throwing herself into his arms and agreeing to everything he had asked of her.

8

Chapter Eight

It had taken a while for her to get there, but she had finally made her choice and she couldn't wait to speak to Justin. Six months was a long period of time to leave someone waiting, and she dearly hoped he would understand.

There never was going to be any other decision but to be with Justin. It had taken her a long time to realise there was no escaping her destiny. She still worried it may be a mistake to give up on her newly found freedom, but Justin had assured her he would not make her do so, and she had to trust him. After all, what was happiness without trust? She had a plan to ensure they both got what they wanted, and she hoped with all her heart that he would agree with her wishes.

Her planning had been meticulous and extensive to arrange this meeting in London with Justin. After all of the thoughtful and delightful gifts he had sent to her, she felt it was only fair to make this joining the most memorable and special possible. She owed him that. He had been nothing but caring towards her since they had reconnected, and this occasion would give her the opportunity to show him what her true feelings were.

The movement in the outer room reminded her of her last preparations, and there was not a moment to lose.

The handle of the bedroom door creaked at it was turning. Anna held her breath, waiting for the sounds of Justin's arrival but everything was silent except for her beating heart, fluttering like a hummingbird's wings.

"Anna."

"Master J."

She shivered as a gentle breeze teased her skin and she felt him stand close to her. He touched her cheek and she lifted her head. He held a letter in one hand and took hold of hers with the other and guided her to her feet.

"Are you not pleased with my presentation, Master J?"

"Of course I am, my love. But I fear this is not what you really want."

Anna laughed as she regarded the face she had thought of every day for so long. "Did you read my letter?"

"Yes," he said, smiling back at her. "I did indeed. I was overjoyed to receive it."

"Then you have also read my suggestions."

"I have."

"But you don't agree with them?"

He pulled her into his arms and cradled her head against his chest. His warm and familiar scent calmed her, although the excitement of the moment added to her determination to achieve her dream. She willed her breathing to slow down while the feel of his body so close to hers had her pulse racing. Despite her earlier confidence, now that he was here, she was terrified she had made a mistake and left him hanging for too long. Or worse, he could not live with the agreement she was proposing. She looked down and saw her letter, abandoned on the floor next to them. She knew she would be all right should he decide not to accept her proposition, but even the thought he would deny her the chance wasn't something she wanted to contemplate.

His arms tightened around her, breathing deeply as he rested his chin on her head. *Why is he not speaking?*

As he lifted his head, he took in a breath and tilted her chin upwards. "Still the little rebel. You were always able to surprise me, and this time is no exception."

She pondered his expression with hope. "But this particular surprise pleases you?"

"I cannot pretend I wasn't intrigued when I received your correspondence. I believed you could not accept that I would honour your wishes regarding your independence."

"But what do you think now, Justin?"

His lips softly touched hers, sending tingles across her skin. "Before I answer that, I want to know if this is truly your wish, or are you merely trying to please me?"

Anna reached up and stroked his face. "It is true I wish to please you, however I also hope for the best of lives. One that I never could have imagined. And now I know what that life could entail, thanks to you, my dearest Justin."

"Just to be clear and in the interests of having no miscommunication—what you are proposing is a partnership where we each can make our own decisions, and maintain our own property, but our intimate life will satisfy both our particular needs and proclivities?"

"Yes, my love. That is what you suggested the last time we were together, and I have spent six months thinking long and hard on how that could work."

"I remember. However, it appears I was not clear enough. What you are proposing is an arrangement. What I dearly wish with all of my being, is to claim you as my wife in front of the entire world. Anna, my love. I want to marry you. I have lived too long without you in my life, and I want to make sure, once and for all that we will always be together."

"But..."

He placed a finger over her lips. "Shh and listen while I explain."

She closed her mouth and stayed silent, but that did not mean she would acquiesce to his wishes. She would make him understand once he had said his piece. It was the only way.

Justin found the silk robe she'd left hanging over a chair and held it out for her to cover herself. He then gestured for her to sit on the leather ottoman at the end of the large bed. Once she was settled, he sat beside her.

"The first thing I want to say is that I love you, and I think you are the bravest and strongest woman I know. I did not believe I would ever get the chance to find you again, so this last nine months has been both delightful, and terrifying, while you were deciding our fate together."

He took her hand, bringing it to his lips and kissed her fingers, one by one. "Justin..."

"Please let me finish, my love."

She could feel the heat of his body next to hers, and as

much as it was distracting, she needed to stay on course. For both their sakes. "As you wish, but I will need to answer your speech with one of my own."

"Of course," he said. "That is only fair."

"Good. As long as we are clear. Please continue."

He laughed. "I have missed your forthrightness, dearest Anna. You always find a way to make me smile. But I digress."

He stood at the window, staring out at the night sky and the streetlamps below. "I know you are concerned that your freedom is at stake, and I understand how much that means to you. I discovered these 'proclivities', as you call them, when I as in Europe and they have suited me for so many years. But for you, I would gladly give them up if you would agree to be my partner and my love for the rest of our lives. Our friendship and love means more to me than anything else."

He walked across the room, kneeling in front of her and grasping her hands.

"Anna. My love. If you agree to marry me, it will be a full partnership. We will share everything, but you can keep your beautiful cottage and your own money, and I will continue to use my London townhouse and manage my own business affairs. We can live in either home, or both—if that is what you wish. Please say you will agree to be my wife."

"But what will others think of you giving me so much freedom, when society dictates a wife's place is to obey her husband? The laws of England state this."

"I care not for what others think of me. My attendance at Maitland House is a prime example. What we do in the confines of a legal marriage is our own business. If we were to continue our relationship without that protection, then we put ourselves in danger of becoming victim to those disgusting indecency laws."

"So that is why you want to marry me? To protect both of us from the laws?"

Justin reached out and kissed her on the lips. Her eyelids closed and the emotions welled up inside her. He deepened the kiss, and she felt his love pouring into her as he drew back, she opened her eyes and saw her dreams reflected in his.

"My love, does that feel as though I want to marry you only to protect you? How can I convince you that it is you that I want, and I intend to shout it to the world without any restrictions?"

Her heart leapt for joy, however her mind, which too often exercised an excess of thinking, and which could be to her detriment, told her to hesitate and be wary. "I do not doubt your intentions, Justin. And I do believe that you believe what you say. But marriage is very final, and the law takes the side of the husband. What if someone was to report us to the authorities?"

His hands dropped back to her lap, clasping her hands once more. He surprised her by smiling. His beautiful eyes sparkled and that dimple she had loved so much when she was young, creased his cheek. "I expected that you may have those doubts, so I put in a contingency plan."

"What contingency plan could stop a husband from demanding his rights?"

He shook his head. "Tsk, tsk. So little faith."

"I am so sorry, Justin," she said.

"I am not offended my love. I know you have had very little experience with trust. This is why you derived so much pleasure from Maitland House. It is in giving over of trust that you are truly free. So here I am, on my knees, asking you to give me yours."

In her heart she believed him. If only that tiny niggle at the back of her mind would dissipate. But what if it was her parents whispering to her from the grave to stay with them again? Should she listen to them after they'd ruined her life and her chances for happiness so long ago? No. She should not. Sitting straighter, with determination now fuelling her, she curled her fingers around his hand and squeezed gently. "I will not let thoughts of my parents influence my decisions anymore."

"That's the Anna I remember."

"If I am to give you my trust, freely and without constriction, then I don't need to know of your contingency."

"Thank you, my love. However, I am sure it will weigh on your mind so I will show you, so there will have no more doubts."

"Justin..." she implored.

He reached into his pocket, drew out a letter and handed it to her.

"What is this?" she asked.

"You may read it, but the gist of it is that I absolve myself of any right to your property, and living arrangements should we marry. It is duly signed, witnessed by my solicitor and a copy is kept in his safe. It is my dearest hope we will never need it, but should something happen to us, this document will ensure your wishes are followed."

A tear trickled down her cheek and a soft sob escaped. "You would do this for me, Justin?"

He pulled her to him and enveloped her in his arms. His warm breath tickled her neck as he kissed that sensitive place behind her ear. "Of course, Anna. Have you not heard a word I have said? You mean more to me than anyone else in this life."

"But what of your intimate leanings? The bedroom?"

"As I said, we will leave them behind if that is what you want."

"But what if I do not wish to leave them behind?"

Justin's quick intake of breath took her off guard and she jumped as he pulled her to her feet.

"What did you say?"

She smiled up at him. "I said— what if I do not wish to forego your special desires?"

"You speak the truth?"

"My time with you at Maitland House was shocking, but the most surprising thing was how much pleasure I found. With all my heart wish there to be no more lies or deceptions between us Justin, so yes—I do speak the truth." She cupped his cheeks and raised up on her toes and kissed him gently. "Why do you think I arranged this hotel room and was waiting naked?" She was so close to him she could feel his swift intake of breath teasing her mouth.

He laughed and kissed her, the fresh scent she had come to think of as his, and his alone filled her senses and her heart. She pulled back, grinning up at him and sliding her arms around his neck. "I think I love you too, my darling man," she whispered, her voice catching.

He lowered his head and kissed the side of her neck, while he moved a hand to the small of her neck and gently stroked her cheek. "It's time for you to stop thinking, and for us to reacquaint ourselves," he whispered against her skin. "It has been an eternity since we were together."

She shivered, turning her head to give him better access. "I think that can be arranged," she whispered. "I might need some prompting though. This could take a while until I'm convinced this is the life for me."

He smiled before laying her down and stretching out beside her on the bed. "We have all the time in the world, my beloved."

She gasped as his lips grazed a trail from her neck to her mouth. The kiss they shared was both gentle and intense. He showed her exactly how much he loved her. The heat between them grew as their bodies moved together, touching each other with abandon. He clasped her hands and raised them above her head. She opened her eyes and watched every move he made, every touch of her skin, every caress of her body, every whisper of his telling her in no uncertain ways how he had missed her.

Her body arched as his mouth captured one breast and sucked before tugging with his teeth. He brought one hand down to squeeze her neglected nipple, twisting and torturing her as her loud sighs urged him on.

"Oh God," she gasped, reaching for his mouth again. She kissed him softly, pouring out all of those emotions and the love she'd kept inside for so many years.

He continued to worship her body, tapping a delicate trail across her skin with his index finger, until he finished at that sensitive area between her legs, sliding into her warmth. She sighed when he added another finger, twisting and sliding back and forth, scissoring his fingers to stretch her in readiness for him.

"I need you," she whispered. "You are the man I have always dreamed of and never forgotten."

"I too have dreamed of you my whole life my love, and the reality is so much better, don't you think?"

"Oh, my goodness! Justin!" He was everything. His scent, his taste, and his talented fingers demanding she give it all to him.

He covered her mouth when she shouted his name, and she forgot how she was meant to breathe. She opened her legs, and he removed his hand, scraping his thumb over her special place He entered her for the first time and her muscles tightened around him. She cried out, surprised at how wonderful it felt.,

He stopped moving "Are you well, my love? Am I hurting you?"

"No, you aren't hurting me! Please, don't stop."

Her breath caught when he moved, and she tensed, revelling in the increasing tempo.

He whispered against her lips, his hot breath fuelling the growing heat inside her. "You are mine."

She groaned, gripping his shoulders, and digging her fingers into his skin. She had never before been so close or so connected with a man, and it felt wonderful" "I am yours forever."

"Does this mean the answer is yes?"

"Yes, Master J."

"Yes!" he shouted. "Thank God!"

His words increased her pleasure, and she couldn't hold

on for much longer, her explosive orgasm tipping him over the edge until he rode along with her, giving himself to her in a way only lovers could.

When their breathing slowed, she caught his face in her hands and kissed him. "Thank goodness we found each other, and I was *Awakened*. I didn't know intimacy could be like this. So peaceful and happy."

"I agree, my love. But I'm nowhere near finished getting intimate with you. Can you take some more?"

Her eyes twinkled. "Oh yes, my Master J. I certainly can."

He laughed and proceeded to teach her what he really meant by intimacy.

And it was better than any wicked or erotic book she had ever read.

2

GEMMA

9

Chapter One

London, 1895

Gemma Hudson felt heat rise from inside her body and spread over her skin. The sight in front of her was so shocking and so unexpected, most definitely something she had never witnessed in all her twenty-one years. When she had stumbled on the hidden doorway into this passage, nothing could have prepared her for what she'd see.

The woman lying naked on the bed sighed as she writhed, her white skin a deep contrast against the black silken sheets. Gemma gasped and drew away from the glass that separated her from the scandalous scene. She closed her eyes and crossed herself in the hope that praying to the good Lord and Saint Jerome would save her soul for having witnessed this forbidden sight.

Run!

Her mind knew what she should do, but her feet stayed

152 - MAGGIE NASH

planted in place, refusing to cooperate. She had suspected something was different about the entertainment offered to the guests at Maitland House, but she'd never imagined it would be so wicked. In the few weeks since she and her friend Lucy had been employed here, she'd noticed hints of secret goings- on behind closed doors, but she had not thought much of it. All who lived here had always shown kindness towards her and none had made any improper demands, not even the exceedingly handsome duo she saw before her. Not once had Master Darius or Master Jamie ever so much as hinted at any impropriety towards her. Now she knew why. They were finding their pleasure elsewhere.

The men in question moved around in the room before her. Fearful lest they'd see her through the darkened glass, she shrank back against the wall in the hidden hallway.

She watched, mesmerised, as each of them stood on opposite sides of the narrow cot and lifted the woman's arms behind her head, fastening them with a length of cloth. The woman writhed on the bed as Darius smoothed her auburn curls from her face and placed a mask over her eyes, but the sound coming from her mouth was not fearful. More a contented sigh of pleasure, thought Gemma as she fidgeted. She fanned her face as unfamiliar sensations stirred her body and she realised there was a dampness between her thighs she could not explain.

As a lady's maid to her best friend Lucy in her former employment, she had lived a very sheltered existence. Her mistress was as innocent as she in the ways of the flesh, and as she had been sent away from her home to work as soon as she was old enough, she had not been blessed with a mother to explain things to her. Lucy's mother had died in childbirth and that witch of a stepmother was barely older than the two of them. Until this very moment she had not had occasion to want or need an explanation of the more intimate details between a woman and a man...or in this case, two men.

She had a feeling, however, that what she witnessed in front of her was not something a mother taught her daughter. Not unless she was a harlot. And Gemma's mother most definitely had not been a harlot, despite her poverty.

Her mouth opened in a gasp. She watched, unable to tear her eyes away as the young men knelt either side of the bed and each claimed a plump breast with his mouth. She bit her lip to stop any sound passing as she felt another intense tingle between her legs. Oh, my Lord.

Closing her eyes, she tried desperately to shut out the sinful scene, but failed, instead seeing herself on that bed, naked and restrained, with both men suckling her breasts. Her hands slid over the tight layers of her gown, and she pinched her nipples through the thick fabric. She tweaked them gently at first, imagining Darius' and Jamie's mouths touching her, then harder as her body reacted to the intense pain and pleasure that ensued.

How could it be that she was here watching this act unfold, touching herself in this way, or that those soft cries of pleasure she heard were this time coming from her lips? It was not what a proper young woman ought to do. Though she was only a scullery maid, she had been a lady's maid and should know better. But instead of guilt for such perverted behaviour, she felt an incredible pleasure far beyond what she had ever imagined.

I am wicked.

"Yes, yes. You are a good student, my dear," said a male voice, startling her.

She opened her eyes in shock. She breathed out, relieved to realise that the voice referred to the woman on the bed and not herself. She looked down at her hands, still over her nipples. Oh, God. Dropping her hands, she thanked all that was holy that the men had not heard her soft cries.

"Our guest deserves a reward for her studious behaviour. What do you think, Jamie?" said Darius.

"Oh yes. I believe you are quite correct, my friend. I have just the thing," he said, smiling.

"By all means. I believe it is your turn to finish off. I cannot wait to see what your wicked brain has in mind." Darius chuckled as he went to the side of the room.

Jamie smiled and sauntered to the end of the cot. He smoothed his large hands along the creamy skin of the woman's legs, then one by one bent them back, her knees brushing her breasts. He slid his hands under her bare buttocks and tugged her body to the edge of the mattress. Her arms strained against the ties as her body slid downward and her head turned to the side, a hint of a smile on her face.

Gemma inched forward, her face so close to the glass it began to mist over while she angled her head to see what Jamie was doing. Her breathing quickened when he knelt down and placed his mouth on the woman's exposed sex. She trembled, moving her hand over the skirt of her gown, inching it upward before she slipped a shaking hand inside her drawers. What would it feel like to have a man touch her so?

"More. I want more, Jamie," the woman cried.

Jamie lifted his head and chuckled. "She is getting too demanding, Darius."

Gemma sighed and closed her eyes, searching for some unknown place inside her that called out for something, pleading to soothe an ache she had no idea how to relieve.

"Yes, she is asking for a punishment. Don't you agree?" said Darius.

"Please, please don't, sir!"

"Please don't...what?" Jamie traced a finger along the plump lips of her sex.

The woman moaned and wrenched at her restrained hands, pulling desperately against the ties. "Please don't punish me, sir. I did not mean to be disrespectful."

Jamie chuckled. "Ah, but all the same you did say it." He spread her nether lips open with the thumb and forefinger of one hand then slapped her across her sex with the other. The woman screamed.

Gemma jumped at the sharp sound of skin hitting flesh. Her hand slid further inside her drawers and she was surprised to find even more dampness than before. Why did the thought of being slapped across her sex make her sweat? She should have been repulsed.

She was not.

"Darius, you should feel this." Jamie added another finger to the two already pleasuring the woman. "She loves this. See how her quim weeps for us."

Darius stepped closer to stand beside the cot. He leant forward and traced a long manicured finger across her entrance. "Delicious," he said, smiling as he stood back and sucked the glistening moisture from the tip. "She is indeed a naughty girl."

The woman moaned again, a tiny sigh escaping her lips each time she breathed. "Please, sir. Please do something."

"I think she needs another lesson, my friend."

"Indeed." Darius nodded. "You may proceed."

"Please, I beg you," cried the woman.

"Do you wish to stop this session, my lady?" Jamie removed his hands from her body and leaned close to her face. "You have only to say the word and this all finishes."

"Oh, God in heaven, no," she cried. "I want you to finish it. I want you to finish it now!"

Jamie smiled at Darius, who returned to the side of the room and nodded. "Then finish it I shall." Jamie thrust two fingers inside her.

"Oh, God!" The woman's body strained to lift off the mattress, but her restraints held her fast.

"Stay still," Jamie snapped.

The woman fell back against the mattress while he continued to move in and out of her sex, sliding back and forth.

The only sounds Gemma could hear were the urgent moans from the woman, each one becoming louder every second, and the slick sound of wet skin on wet skin as fingers slipped back and forth, in and out of the woman's channel.

Of their own volition, Gemma's fingers found their way inside her own entrance and followed the same rhythm that Jamie employed with his guest.

"Oh, God." The strangled cry was loud to her ears but it faded to nothing as the strange feelings inside her continued to build higher and higher. She closed her eyes again, leaning against the wall as the built-up pressure burst and stars appeared across her closed eyelids. Wave after wave of pleasure consumed her as moisture trickled a path from her sex down her thighs. Bewildered, she withdrew her hand from her drawers and attempted to right her tumbled skirt with shaking hands.

"Don't pull down your skirt on my account," breathed a masculine voice close to her ear.

Her eyes flew open. Her heart hammering loudly in her chest, she stared into the shadowed hallway in the direction of the voice. Although she could not see who spoke, she opened her mouth to respond. No sound came out. Oh, Lord. That voice crying out must have been hers. Someone had heard her calling out and she was really in trouble this time. Lucy always told her that her curiosity would be the death of her one day, and now that day had arrived.

As the man drew closer she could see only the dark shadow outlining his imposing size. A familiar scent enveloped her. It smelt of citrus and male but her memory failed to give her a name.

"Give me your hand," the voice demanded.

She stood upright and glanced down at her outstretched hand in confusion. Why was she obeying this stranger? Did she know him?

"That's right, Gemma. Give me your hand, and do it now."

Oh Lord, he knows who I am! Before she had a chance to retreat, his warm hand gripped her wrist and he pulled her closer, giving her a view of his face.

"Master Darius," she whispered. She looked into the stern expression on Darius' face and stopped struggling against his firm hold. She needed the chance to offer an explanation. She didn't want to jeopardise her employment by refusing his orders, and there was something in the way he spoke that compelled her to obey him. She wanted to obey him. And why did the sound of his commands send shivers across her already sensitive skin?

Darius smiled, his blue eyes sparkling in the candlelight as if he knew exactly what she was thinking. Keeping a firm grasp of her wrist, he raised her hand towards his face. Before she knew what he was doing he leant forward, breathing in deeply.

"What do you want with my hand, Master Darius?" she whispered.

"To confirm my suspicions, of course, my lovely Gemma."

She swallowed hard and lowered her eyes. "Suspicions, sir?"

"I believe you saw something you should not have seen," he said, his face shuttered.

Her face burned. *He knows.* There seemed little point in hiding the truth so she remained silent.

He smiled. "I also believe that you touched yourself."

Oh, Lord. She stared at the floor, her body shaking at the thought of one of her superiors being privy to her wicked thoughts and the wanton things she had done.

"I d-did not mean to w-watch, sir. I found this hallway by accident."

"And did you mean to pleasure yourself also?"

Oh, Lord, send a thunderbolt to strike me down here where I stand. She wrenched her hand back and ran down the hallway away from his laughter as fast as she could. She did not know where she would end up, but anywhere was better than the embarrassment of staying.

"Do not leave until I say you can leave," he said.

At the sound of his voice she stopped, but didn't dare turn her head to face his scorn.

Darius threw back his head and laughed. "You are perfect."

Gasping, she turned her head back to find his clear blue eyes staring at her. She did not see any scorn, only curiosity. "Perfect?"

"Oh yes," he replied. "You will do very nicely indeed."

* * *

Darius Wellesley stood to attention before the Master and owner of Maitland House and waited for permission to speak. As the Master of the house, Alexander Sakaroff was also mentor to Darius and a number of his staff, including his friend Jamie Buchanan. Both were there to gain knowledge in the carnal arts and indulge in their proclivities. Since the new queen had been crowned and had imposed her conservative views on society, indulging in the forbidden had become a very attractive pastime. For those with the business acumen and ability to ensure discretion such as Alexander, it could also be very lucrative.

Not that Darius and Jamie needed money. Both were second sons from wealthy families and both possessed generous inheritances. Neither needed to seek business opportunities nor did they require a rich heiress to support them. However, the expertise acquired from the Master would be of great benefit in finding and keeping a mistress should they wish to do so. For the present, they were at Maitland House to experience life until such time as their families insisted they settle down.

At twenty-five, Darius envisaged that the command to wed would not happen for some time. He hoped not as he was enjoying himself entirely too much to give up his hedonistic life just yet.

The Master looked up from his papers, his imposing shoulders stretched tight against the silk of his evening dress shirt. "You have a report on your session with Lady Anne?" he asked, his faint accent betraying his Eastern European heritage.

Darius bowed slightly before smiling at his mentor. "It went very well indeed. She is very pleased, as no doubt will her husband be when she returns to his care."

The Master smiled. "Very good, and you were able to rid her of her affliction?"

"Most definitely. Many times over. She shall have no further fear of her husband's accusations of hysteria, my lord."

"You have done well, Darius." He opened a drawer and withdrew a leather-bound book, placing it in front of him on his desk. "Given your success today, I will assign you another client."

"If I may be so bold, sir, I would like to explore another type of pleasure first before being given extra responsibility."

"Indeed?" The Master cocked an eyebrow. "Why do you feel you need further instruction?"

Darius placed his palms on the desk and lowered his voice. "I would like to explore the voyeur, sir."

The Master smiled, his eyes lighting with humour. "Ah...yes, there are many pleasures in the act of watching, or being watched. I would have thought you did not need instruction in this particular activity."

Darius shifted forward. "I do have some ideas, sir, but I ask permission to test them on one of the servants first before applying my skills to a paying customer."

"And you have a particular servant in mind?"

Darius smiled. "Yes, I do, sir. Do you remember the new scullery maid who came to us this last month?"

The Master sat back in his chair, a momentary flash of emotion in his eyes. "Not Lucy then?"

"No, not Lucy, sir." Interesting that the Master was worried about Darius' choice. He would store that little titbit of information for later. "The young girl I seek is the little redhead who accompanied her. I believe her name is Gemma. She has displayed what might be called a certain aptitude for this activity."

His shoulders relaxed. "Ah, Gemma. Has she consented to the lesson?"

"I believe she will."

"Meaning you have not yet asked her? I will not have anyone involved in lessons against their will."

"I am confident she will consent, sir. However, you have my word as a gentleman that I will do naught unless she agrees."

"Very well then. I will allow it as long as you follow the rules of the house."

"I would not have it any other way, my lord. There is, however, one more aspect of the lessons I wish to try."

"Yes?"

"I believe the lesson will benefit from some added stimulation."

"You have a wicked mind, Darius. Heaven help the woman who is fool enough to fall for your charms. You wish to have another male present, is this correct?"

"Yes, sir. I would like Jamie Buchanan to participate as a third if that is permissible."

"Very well, as long as Gemma consents. You must keep me apprised of your lessons, and remember, I shall be keeping an eye on young Gemma to ensure she is well."

"I would expect no less from you, my lord." Darius bowed. "I will bid you goodnight now, sir."

The Master smiled. "Sleep well, my young apprentice. I believe you have a busy day ahead of you."

Darius left the room, finding Jamie in the hallway.

"Did he agree?" asked Jamie.

Darius smiled. "Yes."

Jamie chuckled. "Thank goodness. Since you made the suggestion my cock has been as stiff as a fencepost. I don't think I can look at the lass again without almost shooting my load."

Darius laughed. "You need a lesson in control, my friend. We need to prolong the pleasure, not finish it before it begins. But first, shall we celebrate with a good brandy while we plan our session?"

"I thought you would never ask."

10

Chapter Two

Gemma raced up the servants' stairs and back to her room. Her heart continued to pound against her chest and her lungs hurt with each breath. As she closed the door, she leaned against the cold wood and slid down to the floor, legs outstretched.

Oh my Lord, what have I done?

She closed her eyes, her body shaking, and wondered what she would do now. It was highly likely that she would be asked to leave Maitland House. After being caught sneaking around the chances of being allowed to stay were minimal. If she were the Master, she would dismiss herself. Squeezing her hands into tight fists she realised her days in employment were most certainly coming to an end. How would she keep herself out of the workhouse now? No doubt she would not be furnished with a reference, given her scandalous behaviour, so her choices were limited.

But her future prospects were overshadowed by her reactions to what she had done. Her body still throbbed at the memory of what she had witnessed—oh, the things she had seen! She closed her eyes as her face heated again, knowing with certainty that she would have stayed and watched for longer had Master Darius not interrupted her. She would have continued to touch herself, feeling sensations she had never before thought possible.

Sensations she still felt. Loosening her clenched fists, she placed her palms on the floor and pushed upright. She removed the cotton cap from her hair and pulled out the few pins holding it in place, shaking the unruly mop of auburn curls free.

Oh, Lord. Not only had she been caught watching a sinful act, but Darius knew she had touched herself. He knew she had felt things and even worse...that she had liked it! How could she ever face him again?

As she undid the ties of her apron and dress she thought of her friend Lucy and how much she was going to miss her. How would Lucy ever forgive her for making a mess of things, or for her stupidity?

She finished removing her remaining clothes and reached for the silk robe hanging on the rack next to her bed. The soft silk slid seductively across her cheek as she held the garment to her nose to inhale the sweet smell of the lavender pouch she always kept in the pocket. The gown had been a gift from Lucy in happier times and she treasured the luxury of the beautiful material. Slipping into the gown, she drew the sides tightly across her middle and tied the belt firmly around her waist, thinking about how her life had changed since leaving the Hall.

A lone owl hooted, drawing her attention to the window. She opened it, enjoying the moonlight silvering the garden below. The hushed quiet of the tranquil scene did nothing to calm the tumultuous thoughts racing through her head. Her skin tingled, still alive with sensation. She re-positioned her arms, folding them tighter across her belly, rubbing the soft silk against her nipples and setting off renewed responses. The room was stifling from the uncharacteristic warmth of this London summer, but the window was too small to afford decent ventilation.

Thinking that some cool air would help her calm down, she slipped out of the room and down the servants' stairs to the kitchen. That room too was oppressively warm from the fire in the hearth that was never allowed to burn out.

She opened the door to the garden and took a few steps outside. The smells of the herbs and flowers were sweet in the night. She closed her eyes and thought of the garden at the Hall. If she tried really hard she could imagine herself sitting in her quiet corner listening to the birds and the water from the stream, and not here in London where by day the clamour and stench of crowds were commonplace.

The stones under her feet were rough and uneven, so she picked her way through the rose arbour that covered the pathway separating the ornamental garden from the vegetable patch. She sighed as her feet touched the soft grass. Ah...bliss! She spied a wooden bench under an oak tree, sat down and drew in the cool evening air.

Gradually her heart slowed and her breathing returned to

normal as she listened to the quiet of the summer night. Her eyes flickered, opening and closing as she struggled to stay awake. Falling asleep in the garden would be one more black mark against her, but as she was already convinced this would be her last night at Maitland House she did not return to her room. She wanted to enjoy this piece of tranquillity as long as she could. Who knew what the morrow would bring? Perhaps she could return to the village and beg the new mistress of the Hall to give her room and board in exchange for work in the kitchen. The new lady of the Hall, with her newly acquired airs and graces, would love to see Gemma reduced to that state. She knew she would hate it, but given the choice between that and the workhouse, she knew which form of hell she would prefer.

Muffled laughter brought her back to the present. She looked around but could not see anyone else. She didn't want to be discovered, so she moved off the bench and pressed her back against the hedge behind her. She heard the laughter again and realised it was coming from the other side of the hedge. Burrowing deeper in case they walked past her, she parted the leaves slightly, gasping at what she could see with only the moonlight offering a shadowy view of the proceedings.

A man and a woman lay on a blanket in the dark. The woman was on her back, her skirts flung upwards exposing her legs. The man knelt between her legs, his face buried in her sex.

"Marcus, that tickles. " The woman giggled.

The man lifted his head slightly. "Thank God. I thought I wasn't doing it right."

As the man lowered his head again the woman let out a loud squeak. "Oh, I believe you could do it a bit better, sir."

The man grunted, followed by the woman's scream.

Gemma released the branches and stood back. Her body was hot and sweaty, and her nipples painful. She'd been at Maitland House for a month without realising the extent of the debauched behaviour. How had that happened? Thinking back, the whispered giggles among some of the other maids and the frequent disappearances of staff without any apparent consequence made sense to her. Perhaps her employers were waiting for her to discover it all for herself and wanted to see her reaction. The veil was now off her eyes. Everywhere she looked brought her a view of one more erotic scene.

She tried to think of the best way to escape without being noticed, for she had learnt her lesson this afternoon. It would not be prudent for her to stay longer and risk discovery. She could not bear it if Darius found her in such a compromising position again.

Darius stood by his window swirling the brandy in his glass when a flash of movement caught his eye. By the light of the moon he could just make out a reddish glint in the curls of the woman as she hurried to hide in the centre of the hedge.

Interesting.

He continued to watch for a few minutes, but she had yet to reappear.

He smiled. There was no time like the present to start her lessons, he thought. He drained his glass and placed it on the side table near his door as he left the room.

He slipped through the kitchen and reached the garden

scant minutes later. He spied a strip of white poking through the leaves of the hedge. Good, he thought. She was still there. Upon hearing a loud, lusty cry from the other side of the hedge, he knew the reason behind her hiding place.

She really is a naughty girl, he thought. And naughty girls deserve to be taught a lesson.

He walked quietly towards the hedge just as his quarry backed out. He grabbed her upper arms to prevent her colliding into him. "Shh..." he whispered against her ear. "They will hear you."

She struggled against him, rubbing her delectable bottom against his groin, gasping when his erection pressed against her. Good. He wanted her to know that finding her enjoying a carnal act pleasured him.

"Please let me go, sir," she whispered.

He smiled, sensing her arousal. "Why would you want to leave, my dear?" Sliding a hand over her arm and brushing her hair aside, he exposed the white skin of her neck. "Just when it's getting interesting."

She shivered, turning her head to the side. "We shouldn't be watching, sir. It's private."

He nuzzled her neck and placed his lips against the sensitive spot just below her ear. "That's where you are wrong. Unless the activities are in a private room, all is open to be seen here at Maitland House."

Gemma fidgeted, trying to turn to face him. "B-b-but why would anyone agree to th-that? "

He wrapped both his arms around her body, brushing her breasts. "Because, my dear one, this place is about fantasies. Being watched, like watching, is something people enjoy."

"But that is wicked!"

Darius laughed softly. "Some might say so, but do you really believe that to feel pleasure, to live out your deepest fantasies...is wicked?" he said as he cupped her breasts.

Her nipples lengthened. Gemma gasped and wriggled. I...um..." She leaned her body back against his, sighing as her bottom touched his groin.

"Well? I expect an answer, Gemma," he said, tweaking her nipples and squeezing them gently.

She struggled against him and lifted her arms, covering his hands with her own and tugging at them.

But he held firm. "Answer me. Can you honestly say you would forgo pleasure just because society tells you you must?"

She shook her head back and forth. "I don't...I don't really know, sir."

His heart lifted at her response. He was correct in believing she was ready for this. "Very good. An honest answer." He released her nipples and placed his hands on her shoulders, turning her to face him. "Do not ever deny your pleasure or your needs, little one. It leads to many problems, some you would not even dream of."

"But what if some of those needs are not allowed. What of the new laws?"

"You speak of the Labouchere amendment? I am impressed that you are aware of the affairs of the government."

She took a step backwards. "Impressed, sir? Why? Because as a scullery maid I am not expected to read?"

Intrigued with her spirit, he smiled. "Quite frankly, my dear, yes. I have never before met a scullery maid who reads the newspaper."

She looked up, her eyes flashing and her nostrils flaring. "I was not always a scullery maid sir. Before I came to Maitland House I was a lady's maid and companion."

That certainly explained her dignity and her eloquent speech. His interest was truly piqued. "Is that so? And for whom did you fulfil these onerous duties?"

She looked away. "No one of any consequence, sir. You should be more interested in how you keep the constabulary from closing down this household and locking you and the Master away in the Old Bailey."

The sound of more laughter accompanied by footsteps signalled the departure of the couple from the other side of the hedge.

"It seems our friends have left us," he said as he reached up and slipped a stray curl behind her ear. "Do not worry on our account, we are quite safe within these walls. The Master has many friends and clients from the government."

She shivered when he stroked her cheek with the back of his hand. Her skin was as soft as the finest velvet.

"Th-that is very interesting, sir."

He stepped closer, feeling her soft breath against his neck as he rested his chin on the top of her head. "Yes it is, but not as interesting as you, my dear. Now tell me more about your previous life."

Moving her head, she tried to step away, but the hedge impeded her progress. "It's all very boring, sir. I am sure there are others here at Maitland House who are more interesting than I."

He leant forward, speaking softly against her ear. "I can

see you are not ready to trust me yet, little one. But you will in time."

Her shoulders rose as she shivered, despite the summer evening. "Please, sir, I should go back to my room," she whispered. "I am needed in the kitchen in a few short hours."

He sighed, knowing he should not hold her from her duties. "I will let you go when you agree to allow me to gain your trust."

"I do not understand, sir."

"If you will agree to meet with me tomorrow, I will show you more ways to feel pleasure." He placed a finger over her lips. "Before you say no, I will assure you that nothing will happen unless you allow it to. If you ask to stop our lessons, I will honour your wishes."

She stared at him, her face a picture of innocence. "I am not sure what you are asking, sir."

"I want to show you what is possible. I want to teach you not to deny your feelings or that wonderful passion I see beneath your very proper appearance." He kissed her lightly on her forehead, her skin warm and soft against his lips.

She looked away from him, her bottom lip caught between her teeth. "I shouldn't, sir."

He smiled. "But you will."

Still she refused to look at him. "You will let me go if I ask it of you?"

"You have my word as a gentleman."

"Please, sir. May I have this night to think about it?"

He cupped her face with both hands, turning her to face him. "Look at me, Gemma."

She slowly raised her eyes. "Please?"

His face was barely inches from her mouth. Her sweet breath mingled with his as he whispered against her lips. "You have until morning."

She licked her bottom lip.

"Here is something to help you think about it." His mouth covered hers.

He had expected to coax her mouth open, but nothing prepared him for the spark of electricity once their lips met. His tongue licked along the seam of her mouth and she willingly opened for him, allowing him to invade the velvet depths. She sighed as he explored her mouth, flicking in and out slowly and sending heat coursing through his veins. He licked and tongued and suckled her mouth as she leaned into his embrace.

He struggled to withdraw, especially as his cock was as hard as a pole, but he knew the pleasure that awaited them on the morrow was worth some self-restraint now. As he eased away from the kiss, he smoothed his hands down her shoulders and gently pushed her back. Her eyes were burning with need and he almost took her again, but reluctantly held back. "Until tomorrow, little one."

Her breathing was ragged as she stared at him for a few more seconds before walking to the house. He kept watching as she slipped back through the kitchen door, closing it softly behind her.

Only then did he allow himself to adjust his trousers. Tomorrow was going to be an interesting day indeed.

II

Chapter Three

Gemma awoke to a hand gently shaking her shoulder. She opened her eyes and sprang upright.

"Lucy, you scared me half to death!" She relaxed against the mattress.

Her friend chuckled as she sat down on the side of the narrow bed. "You need to wake up, sleepyhead. Cook is looking for you."

Gemma shot back up and scrubbed her face with her hands. "What time is it?"

"It is almost five o'clock. It was your turn to tend the fire." Lucy stood and threw back the covers.

"Oh, Lord!" Gemma climbed out of bed.

"Don't worry, I've tended to it, but we still need to hurry to help Cook prepare the loaves for breakfast."

Gemma searched the open trunk at the foot of her bed for a clean dress and settled on a plain grey gown from her days at the Hall. "This will have to do. I don't have time to find my clean work clothes," she said as she pulled it over her head.

Lucy shook out a starched white apron and held it out for Gemma, who tied it around her waist.

"What would I do without my dearest friend to get me out of trouble yet again?"

"I believe the scales are dipping further on your side of good deeds, Gem, but we don't have time to argue the point right now. Sit down so I can put your hair to rights."

Within minutes, with hair neatly tied back and shoes found, they both headed down the stairs to the kitchen. As they helped Cook to knead the loaves Lucy leaned over and whispered, "When we finish our morning chores I want to hear exactly what it was that had you tossing and turning all night."

Gemma's face burned. Of course her friend would notice something was amiss. She never slept in. It was usually she who was waking her friend, not the other way around. "I don't know if there is anything to tell, " she whispered back.

"From the way your face is flushed I find that hard to be-lieve." Lucy chuckled. "I am sure you will tell me eventually. We always share our secrets."

Yes, we do, she thought. But what would the former Lady Lucinda think if Gemma explained the real reason for her disturbed sleep? She bit her lip, worried she might blurt out what was on her mind. That lip tingled as though remember-ing Darius' kiss. She'd been kissed before, but oh, Lord, Master Darius had to be the most expert kisser she had ever met. Her breasts swelled and she imagined his hands still touching her, except this time her skin was bare, like in her dream.

"Gem?"

"Yes?" In an effort to shake off the fantasy, she rubbed her sleeve against her eyes. Her hands would have been preferable, but given that they were elbow deep in bread dough and flour, she thought better of it. "Sorry, Lucy, "she whispered back. "I was wool-gathering."

Her friend chuckled. "I could tell. If you are still finding it so difficult to work, perhaps you should ask Cook if you may rest for a while."

"No, I will not be a slug-a-bed. Perhaps a glass of water will set me to rights." She wiped her hands, crossed the room to the water pump over the sink and filled a cup. Taking a long drink of cool water helped to focus her thoughts on her duties. Her position might already be in jeopardy after yesterday's events, so neglecting her work would make her situation a lot worse.

Darius was, after all, only a student of the Master. Despite his assurances that she would suffer no consequences for allowing him to tutor her in the pursuits of pleasure, she did not truly trust that to be the case. She needed her job and would not do anything to endanger her position or that of her friend.

However, the temptation to give in to her newly-found carnal needs was great. If Darius showed her more scenes of pleasure, or God forbid, kissed her again, she knew her brain would be befuddled and she would give in to his demands.

With any luck he had forgotten all about her this morning and was pursuing another, so she need not make a decision. The chill of the cool water washing over her fingers as she rinsed the cup reminded her she had chores to complete before any of the guests' activities would take place. She had some time yet should Darius still wish to seek her out. She decided she would think on it later. At this moment she needed to prevent Cook from finding her neglecting her duties.

It would help her appearance of normality if Lucy ceased to worry about her.

"I feel much better now."

Lucy placed the last round of dough into a loaf tin, set it alongside the rest and covered them all with a damp muslin cloth. "Ha! That is fortuitous of you to feel better now that the work is done."

Gemma set to cleaning the table. The sound of the scraping block scooping up the excess flour allowed them to continue their conversation in private. "If your dear father's new wife were to see me now she would feel vindicated in her poor opinion of me."

"I believe she hated me more than you," said Lucy.

"Oh, no. She was threatened by you, Lucy. As the legitimate heir you stood between her and your father's money. As for myself, I dared to stand up to her. She hated me."

"More work, less talk!" Cook lifted the muslin to check on the loaves, her smile belying the harshness of her words. "We have eggs to poach and bacon to slice. You can gossip when your chores are done."

"Yes, Cook," they chorused, separating to complete their allotted duties.

* * *

Darius and Jamie worked together on the morning's tasks with the Master. They had both been assigned to prepare a guest for her first day of training. It never ceased to amaze

Darius how quickly some of these clients let go of their inhibitions. As the young girl accompanied them through the hallways of the house completely naked to all who passed, he reflected on how different this hedonistic life was from his own. These tasks were usually most enjoyable, and in truth the new young girl under the Master's care was proving to be a beautiful distraction.

But Darius' thoughts continually returned to Gemma. In a state of constant hardness, his cock twitched in anticipation of the lessons he planned for her. Initially he had thought only to use her for more practice, but now he could think of nothing but the pleasure she would bring him as she began her journey of discovery, a journey on which he would be very happy to take her.

Her fiery hair and flashing blue eyes had got under his skin. She appeared to be innocent, but the depth of her unrestrained responses left him breathless. Was she even aware of the allure of an aroused woman to a man? He thought not, but he would remedy that situation as soon as he could. When he'd first come to Maitland House it had all been a bit of a lark. He'd developed a fascination for Gemma, so things were getting very interesting.

He finished tending the fire in the Master's study, chuckling to himself as he glanced over at his friend. Jamie was enjoying a quick reward: two minutes to become acquainted with the young girl's cunny. By the end of the day Darius intended to compensate himself in a similar fashion, but that would be only the beginning of the bounty he would soon receive.

Darius checked his watch as he and Jamie left the room.

The Master would be calling for them to return in about an hour, so that gave him a little time to prepare his space and to seek his quarry.

"Has she agreed to your plan yet?" Jamie asked.

"Not as yet, but she will."

"You are very confident, my friend. What if she refuses?"

"She will not. You should have seen her in the garden last night. She is made for this."

Jamie snorted. "You have been wrong before. Remember Daisy Woodruff?"

Darius groaned. "Now that is just cruel. A friend does not remind one of his youthful failures. "They headed down the ornate staircase towards the front hall. "Besides, her sister told me she had a tendre for me. How was I to know her sibling was playing a joke on her?"

Jamie snickered. "I can still see the look on your face when she slapped your cheek. It was hilarious."

"We were only thirteen at the time. I believe I have mastered a thing or two since then," said Darius, smiling as he remembered just how much he had absorbed, and how much more he would learn before he left Maitland House.

"I hope so. I would hate to see you face another rejection. Particularly since you seem to be quite taken with this girl." Jamie slapped Darius on the back.

"I agree, she has captured my imagination," he said as he left the hall and detoured in the direction of the kitchen. "I do not believe I am mistaken this time. She is fascinated with what she has seen over the last day. Although she tries to deny it, especially to herself, she wants to explore this as much as I want to teach her."

"I look forward to it then, my friend," said James. "I'll see you both at the de-sensitising ceremony."

"Oh, yes." Darius grinned. "I am looking forward to introducing our girl to that pleasure." He grasped the door to the kitchen and swung it open.

"Be good to her."

"I intend to be," he said. The staircase creaked as he went to the kitchen. Years of use had worn indentations into each stair from past servants and every single step had a story to tell. The kitchen was hot, heat radiating from the main ovens. A smaller fire burned in the fireplace where a large black kettle was suspended. The hiss of the boiling water drew his attention as he watched the object of his fantasies scoop bubbling liquid into a pot.

He raced to her side. "Be careful, lass." He wrapped his hands around hers to take the weight of the heavy utensil.

"I am perfectly capable of carrying a small pot. This is my job, sir. You should not have startled me, Master Darius, I could have burned you."

What she said was true, but he wanted to protect her. "I do not like to see a lady carrying out a task that could injure her."

"As I said, sir, this is one of my duties. And kindly remember, I am not a lady."

He smiled. "Ah, but you used to be a companion to one."

She stared at him, placed a finger over her lips and whispered, "Please, sir, I would be most grateful if you did not mention that fact to the other staff."

The distress in her eyes gave him pause to question her further, but he decided there would be time for that at a later date. "As you wish. But rest assured I will find out the rest of that story later."

"What if I do not wish to tell you?"

He winked at her. "After you begin to trust me, you will tell me anything."

She laughed. "You are very sure of yourself, sir. How do you know I will agree to your demands?"

"I can see it in your eyes, love. You have already decided."

A loud bell signalled a summons from the Master's study. Gemma looked around as some of the staff giggled and dropped their tools, heading out of the door.

Darius smiled at Gemma and offered his hand. "Come, Gemma. Your lesson is about to start."

"I cannot just leave my duties, sir. There is work to be done. More now that the staff are leaving their chores in droves."

Darius laughed. "They are still completing their duties."

"What duties would they be?" she asked.

"Come with me and you will find out."

"But the Master will be angry if the chores are not done."

"Trust me when I tell you, this is one chore he is happy for his staff to complete."

She hesitated, staring at his outstretched hand for a few seconds longer before giving him her own. He held on fast lest she change her mind and led her to the stairs.

"Where are we going?"

"To the Master's study."

"What are we to do there?"

"You will see when we get there."

"Why can't you tell me now?"

"That would spoil the surprise, my dear. However, I will tell you the rules."

"Rules?" she asked.

"Yes, rules. The Master is very strict about his rules. You must promise me you will obey them completely."

She bit her lip in that delicious habit of hers when nervous. "I will make every effort, sir."

"You will obey."

"I will obey, sir. But first you must tell me what rules I am to obey."

"You are an impudent young lady, but I will let that one pass." He winked at her as they reached the hallway, where a small group of staff and clients were climbing the stairs towards the Master's study.

"First and foremost, you must not speak a word while you are in that room. No matter what you see or what you do, you must not utter a sound. Is that clear?"

"Perfectly, sir."

"The second rule is that you must obey your Master. This is either Master Alexander or myself. Is that also understood? Nod if you understand."

She nodded immediately, her eyes wide with curiosity.

"Good. What you see inside that room will shock you, little one, but it is not too different from what you have seen this past day."

Her eyes showed a hint of fear, but she could not hide the heat as her pupils dilated at his words.

"I see you are lost for words. That is good. I will question you later on your reactions, but for now it is good to keep your thoughts to yourself and just enjoy."

"Enjoy?"

"Oh yes, my dear. You have already proven to me that you find pleasure in watching. You are a voyeur."

"I have read of it, sir. Is it not deviant behaviour?"

"No, pleasure is never deviant. It is completely normal to experience it. You are completely normal."

"I do not know what is normal, sir."

He squeezed her hand as they neared the door. "Do not worry, I do."

The door opened and the Master stood back, ushering them to file inside. "Come in, my friends. Come and meet my guest."

Gemma looked past him and saw a young girl sitting in an armchair, her arms and legs held in place with silk scarves. A blindfold covered her eyes, but her long dark curls spread like a curtain over her shoulders. Her knees were spread apart, and she was completely naked.

Oh, my Lord! Gemma closed her eyes tightly. This had to be a dream. In the real world this sort of scene just did not happen.

A distinguished man walked into the room after all the staff had entered. He was tall and well-dressed in a dark suit. Ignoring the staff, he walked to the far wall and stood against it as if to watch the proceedings.

The Master walked to the girl's side and spoke softly to her. "Do not be afraid. Your face is covered. No one knows who you are." She visibly relaxed, but Gemma did not know how she could remain so calm. She was both horrified and excited by the thought of what would happen if it had been her tied up and laid out for all to see. She should be repelled, but being here with all of these people acting as if nothing was amiss gave her a new perspective. Perhaps Darius was correct and this was a normal activity.

The Master faced the crowd. "Friends, you may begin your inspection."

The girl's intake of breath was loud enough to be heard around the room.

The Master placed his hand on her shoulder. "Hush, you will enjoy this, but if you wish to stop you must tell me now."

The girl breathed in and out a few times. The gentleman at the back of the room began to move towards her but stopped when she spoke, her voice husky and ragged. "No, I want to do this. You may proceed."

"You are sure?" asked the Master.

She spoke again, this time her voice stronger. "Yes, I am sure, Master. Please commence."

The gentleman nodded at the master in some unspoken message and again retreated. The Master stood back and waved his hand in the air towards the girl.

"Ladies and gentlemen, you heard the lady. You may begin."

One by one the staff of five filed past the girl. As each one approached they touched her.

Darius whispered close to Gemma's ear, his warm breath sending shivers across her already sensitised skin. "You may use only your hands to touch."

Before she had time to think, she was in front of the girl. Gemma's heart pounded as she reached out with her index finger and touched the silky soft skin of the girl's cheek.

Her sigh spurred Gemma and she continued her journey to the woman's breast, running the tip of her finger around the nipple until it tightened to a peak. Darius placed a hand on her shoulder alerting her to move on. She watched, mesmerised as the men took turns in pinching the girl's nipples or running their fingers over her hairless crotch.

The Master and the other gentleman watched the girl but didn't join in the activity. Gemma wondered who the gentleman was and what this girl meant to him.

The heady scent of the girl's arousal surrounded them while her breathing became more and more ragged with each touch. From across the room Gemma stared at the girl's exposed body, transfixed, as a tiny trickle of fluid escaped from her sex and glistened on the skin of her upper thighs.

The second round started, but this time the Master instructed them to use their mouths. Gemma stood back, allowing the others to take their turn. She could not yet bring herself to touch another woman in such an intimate fashion. The girl's moans were loud against the silence of the participants as the last of the men—Darius—sucked on her sensitive nub. Her head twisted from side to side as she screamed her pleasure.

Gemma felt a twinge of something akin to jealousy as the girl climaxed. Gemma did not know if she felt this way because it was Darius who touched this woman, or because she wished he was kissing Gemma herself so intimately.

Darius stood and stared at Gemma, his eyes burning with passion as if he had been pleasuring her and not this strange girl.

The Master clapped his hands, gathering everyone's attention. "This session is finished, you may leave. Thank you all for your assistance."

Gemma felt rather than saw Darius' presence beside her as they followed the group down the stairs. When they reached the hall, his hand cupped her elbow and he steered her into a small room off the main hallway, closing the door.

"Excuse me, sir, but I must return to my duties," she said. "I cannot stay here with you."

He shook his head, his blue eyes twinkling. "On the contrary, my dear, the Master has given his approval for you to spend time with me."

She sucked in a breath and started to cough. "He knows you wish to..."

He laughed. "Yes, he knows my intentions with you. Do you mind if I lock the door? I believe you would prefer some privacy."

Her breathing settled into some degree of normalcy. "Um...I suppose so sir."

He closed and locked the door. "Darius," he said.

"Sir?"

"No, not sir. You may call me Darius."

"But it isn't proper for a scullery maid to address you so, sir. Should I not call you Master Darius?"

"For our lessons I would prefer for you to call me Darius. I wish to gain your trust. Calling me by my given name will help facilitate this, so I will forgo outdated social conventions."

She was surprised that this young gentleman would even consider such informality, but she had to agree that she felt more comfortable thinking of him as just plain Darius. If she was to go through with her lessons, and she believed she wanted to, then she needed to trust him. She was more terrified than she had ever been in her life, but despite the fears something else compelled her to stay. She wanted to know what had been awakened in her when she had found herself in that secret hallway watching a woman being pleasured by two men.

Darius walked to the middle of the room and pointed to a love seat. "Sit down, Gemma. We have much to discuss."

She was frozen in place and couldn't move. Maybe she did not want this as much as she believed she did.

"Gemma?" he asked, moving closer to cup her cheek. "Are you well?"

She turned her cheek into his hand, the warmth of his skin calming her. "Yes, Darius, I believe I am."

"Very well then, let us begin."

She took in a large breath and blew it out slowly. Lucy always said her curiosity would get her into trouble, but at least trouble was not boring. She sat down on the edge of the chair, jumping when Darius sat beside her. His body was not touching hers, but she could feel the heat and the male power emanating from him.

"Make yourself comfortable, Gemma," He leant back on the couch and placed his arms across its back. "I promise we will only talk for now."

"For now?"

Her mouth went dry when he smiled at her. "I cannot promise it will only be talk for the whole evening, but for now I want you to tell me about today's exercise."

She shifted in her place, not sure what he expected. "You were there with me. What more is there to tell?"

"We need to discuss your reactions to what you saw. I will

help you." He leaned closer, his warm breath tickling her ear. "Tell me what you felt when you saw the girl."

Her skin heated as she remembered her reaction on arriving in the room. "I do not know what you want me to say."

He wrapped his arm around her shoulder and pulled her closer to him. "Did you imagine yourself in that chair?"

Yes. "Ah..."

"Do your breasts tingle?" He slipped his hand under her arm and rubbed her breast.

Oh, my Lord. These feelings overwhelmed her with frightening ease.

Darius placed his free hand over her other breast and pinched her nipple. "Gemma, I did not hear your answer. Do your breasts tingle?"

"Yes," she whispered.

"Good," he said, and pinched her nipple harder. "Are your nipples tight and painful?"

"Yes, oh yes..."

He removed his hands, leaving her wanting more. "Stand up, Gemma."

She stood obediently and Darius lifted her skirt before she realised what was happening. His hands held her hips in place.

"You are aroused, Gemma."

She shivered, sparking tingles across her skin. She should have been embarrassed, but it felt too good to be wrong.

A long finger slipped inside her drawers, rubbing back and forth across her sex and setting off sensations deep inside her body that she had never before imagined.

He removed his finger and held it up in front of her face.

"Look at the proof of your pleasure, Gemma." Fluids glistened on his finger in the afternoon light.

He held his finger nearer her face. "Smell your arousal," he whispered, his warm breath soft on her cheek.

Her nostrils flared as the musky scent reached her nose.

"Taste it," he said, and slid his finger into her mouth.

The tension that had built up from the last hour suddenly released as she tasted her own juices mixed with the salty flavour of his skin. Her head fell back and she attempted to slow down her ragged breathing.

"I believe I have proved my theory." He smoothed her skirts back into place.

Legs like jelly, she sat. "What theory is that?"

"I think this proves that you very much like to watch."

She managed a smile. "I believe you are correct, sir. Your lesson was most illuminating."

"The lesson is not over yet, little one. Now onwards to prove my other theory."

'What other theory would that be, sir?"

He stood up and reached out for her hand, helping her to stand. "We know that you like to watch. Come with me now and we will find out if you like being watched."

The air left her lungs and she felt faint. He could not mean to pleasure her in front of others? Could she possibly allow him to touch her body with others watching?

"Do not think too much, little one. You know that you wished it was you on display there in the Master's study."

She struggled to speak but air refused to go into her lungs. Finally she sucked in a breath and said, "Wishing and doing are not the same thing."

He smiled at her. "Remember that all wishes and fantasies can and do come true here at Maitland House."

She was wavering, and it seemed he knew it, judging by the smug expression on his handsome face. "I am not so sure."

He took her hand in his and headed for the door. "You may stop it at any time."

* * *

Darius led Gemma to the place in the garden he had prepared earlier. A high hedge enclosed this section, creating a private but open space. A large oak tree stood in the centre of the clearing, shading it from the summer sun.

She was skittish and he feared that she might not go through with it. He needed to work quickly and led her to the tree.

She hesitated. "What are you going to do?"

He smiled at her, stroking her face to soothe away the lines of worry around her mouth. "I am going to bring you great pleasure."

She turned her head side to side. "But where are the others?"

"I felt it would be better to ease you into this. To earn your trust one step at a time."

He directed her to stand with her back against the tree. "You are beginning to trust me, aren't you?"

Her eyes widened and she nodded, so he placed a scarf over her eyes and tied it at the back of her head.

"You are very quiet, little one. Do you wish to continue?"

She hesitated, taking in a deep breath before speaking. "Yes, I think so."

"You think so? Or you are sure?"

Her voice became firmer, more confident as the freedom of the blindfold took over.

"Yes, I am sure."

He let out a breath, relieved she was still willing, for his body was ready to explode. He wanted her. No other woman would suffice. "Then we shall begin. Relax and enjoy. I know that I will."

"Thank you, Darius."

He laughed. "It will be my pleasure."

He removed her apron first, reaching behind her to untie the bow before tossing it on the grass. "I need you to keep very still while we get ready, and try not to speak unless you wish me to stop. Is that understood?"

She nodded.

"Excellent."

He took his time removing her gown. As each tiny button was unfastened, more of her pale skin was revealed. When he reached her waist he pulled the rest of the gown to her ankles and lifted her feet one by one to remove it completely.

Seeing Jamie at the edge of the clearing, Darius beckoned his friend, who started to remove Gemma's underskirt.

She shivered and goose pimples appeared all over her skin.

Darius moved closer and brushed her lips with his own. "Are you well, little one?"

She sighed into his lips and nodded.

"You are doing very well. I am very pleased," he said just before kissing her again. She smiled against his lips and his heart jumped. Stepping back, he waited while Jamie lifted her chemise, forcing her arms over her head to release it. Before her arms could drop, he wrapped a silk rope around each wrist, tying her arms around the tree. Her soft sigh was the only indication that she was affected by this sudden move.

While Jamie took off her drawers, Darius stood back to admire her lush body.

"You are a work of art, my dear Gemma."

"She certainly is," Jamie said.

Gemma gasped and lost her balance, falling against the ties.

As Jamie held her arm and helped her regain her footing, Darius cupped her face with both hands. "Take a deep breath, little one. This is what you wanted, is it not?"

She did as he told her and breathed out slowly, reacting to his soothing words.

"Well done. You are now ready to begin."

Gemma fought the urge to call out and stop the proceedings. She could feel her pulse pounding inside her head. What had she agreed to? She was here in daylight tied naked to a tree in view of anyone who walked by.

"Are you still well, little one?"

Darius' soothing voice calmed her nerves. She had come this far, she would finish it. "I am frightened, Darius," she whispered. "But I want to continue."

"Good," he said and kissed her. He clasped her hair in his hands and pulled her head back, allowing him to deepen the kiss. His tongue swept in and out in a rhythm that sent an arc of sensation directly to her core. A mouth covered one of her breasts and she gasped against Darius' mouth. He pulled back and whispered against her lips, "Do not worry. It is Jamie who touches you. I trust him."

She did not know where to concentrate her thoughts. The kiss was beautiful but the feeling of a mouth suckling her breast was taking her breath away. As if he read her thoughts, Darius left her mouth and kissed a trail down her throat and all the way to her other breast and began suckling in unison with Jamie.

Her head fell back against the tree as she basked in the sensations. She burned from the inside out, certain that she was going to ignite.

A hand cupped her sex and she shivered.

A voice whispered in her ear. "You cannot see, but there may be others watching you, enjoying the feast that is your body."

Oh, God! If she had not been tethered to the tree she would have fallen to the ground.

The hand moved, and a finger caressed her folds before sliding inside her. She gasped at the invasion. Only her own small finger had been there before and never as deeply as this.

"Do you feel me moving inside you, Gemma?"

"Yes," she whispered, surprised that her voice worked at all.

A second finger joined the first, twisting back and forth. They felt strange, but not unpleasant. In fact the longer they remained, the more the sensations magnified.

A pair of hands moved her legs apart and spread her open.

Beneath the mask she closed her eyes and gasped. Warm breath blew against her entrance and the fingers inside her withdrew.

"Look at her pretty quim. It is quite beautiful, don't you agree?"

"Oh yes, quite delectable." A stranger's voice.

She almost fainted.

"Do not worry, my dear. Just relax and enjoy."

Her feelings were tied into knots. She tried to comply with Darius' advice but that became impossible when a mouth latched on to her cunny.

"Please come closer, my friends, and watch my little one as she learns about pleasure."

Two hands squeezed her breasts as the fingers returned inside her and the mouth continued feasting between her legs. Someone turned her head to the side and kissed her, an agile tongue darting in and out of her mouth.

She dragged her mouth away as she forced breath into her lungs. The tension in her body was coiled like a spring.

"She tastes wonderful," said the voice near her sex. "And she nears her climax,"

"It is time then," Darius said.

All touching stopped and she panted, desperate for completion but unworried about being so exposed.

"Please..."

"Do you wish to stop?"

"No, I want more," she shouted.

Darius laughed as she felt him grasp her hips. "Then you shall have more."

She felt the head of his cock against her entrance and moved her hips to meet him.

"You are beautiful." He pushed slowly inside her tight cunny, but stopped partway in. "Are you well?"

"It feels strange, but I am well, Darius."

"I am glad because I don't believe I can stop now," he said as he pushed deeply inside her in one quick movement.

She gasped at the sudden sting, not sure if she could continue. Her muscles contracted.

Darius stayed still, his breath heavy on her neck as he rested his head on her shoulder.

As the stinging sensation subsided he began to move in and out, slowly at first, but increasing the rhythm as her muscles relaxed around him. She trembled as the sensations built, thrilling her as Darius flexed one last time and filled her. Her body exploded around him as her hands were released. She flung her arms around his shoulders and hugged him close.

Still inside her, he removed the blindfold. She blinked and looked around, crying out in surprise. "There is no one here."

Darius smiled at her. "I sent them away."

"But why?"

"I thought you deserved your first time to be private."

She smiled back, kissing him lightly on the lips. "Thank you."

"My pleasure." He eased himself out, lifted her in his arms and carried her towards the house.

"And that, my dear, proves my third theory."

"There was a third theory?"

"Of course. I have proven to you that sometimes it is only the thought of being watched that is enough. A good theory, don't you think?"

"Oh, yes, sir. Most illuminating."

About the Author

Maggie Nash writes what she loves to read, and as her reading tastes change, so does her writing. She has written books across many different genres, including romantic suspense, erotic tales of domination and submission, contemporary action adventure, dark historical romance and thrillers. She also writes contemporary and fantasy as Maggie Mitchell.

Maggie lives in Sydney, Australia and there is nothing she enjoys more than a good coffee and a great book

9 780645 365221